Junior—

Use this journal to record what you see and learn.

Regards,

Father, April 1908

THE FEDERAL SECURITY SERVICE OF THE RUSSIAN FEDERATION

DATE:
December 10, 19████
May 22, 20███

TO:
"Mad Dog,"
 Research Department for External Intelligence, North Korea;
"Monkey," America Department (DA),
 Communist Party of Cuba Centra Committee, Cuba
"Grey Wolf,"
 Ministry of State Security (MSS), China

Translated from the Russian for our Korean, Chinese,
and Cuban comrades.

        ****

This journal was removed from one Dr. Henry Jones, Jr. in
November 1957, and we are pleased to have it as part of our
impressive collection. Of note, the journal chronicles the
career of Dr. Jones, who was known as a collector of ancient
artifacts. Further research indicates that he was also called,
among other monikers, "adventurer," "graverobber," "Junior,"
and "playboy."

        ****

The items of interest enclosed therein include:

-Information about Dr. Jones's youth, including encounters
with the man we now know as Lawrence of Arabia, American
president Theodore Roosevelt, and Mexican revolutionary Pancho
Villa.

-Dr. Jones's experiences fighting for the Belgian army in
World War I.

-An unexpected journey to Mayapore Village in India, leading
to seemingly unpleasant encounters with members of the Thuggee
Cult at Pankot Palace.

-Professorship evaluations and corrected papers of little
interest to us.

-Sketch of Golden Idol that Dr. Jones does not seem to have
successfully recovered.

-Accounting of a journey to Nepal and Egypt involving a
medallion and one Marion Ravenwood.

-Torn pages from a diary owned by one Henry Jones, Sr.,
[Dr. Jones's father] and chronicling the whereabouts of
"The Holy Grail."

-Reference to Dr. Jones's time as a soldier during WWII.

-Studies on the Amazon and Hangar 51.

-Diagrams of "The Cross of Coronado," "The Chachapoyan
Temple," "The Peacock's Eye," "The Ark of the Covenant,"
and "The Holy Grail," among others.

****

Among Dr. Jones's known associates are Marcus Brody, Abner
Ravenwood, Wilhelmina "Willie" Scott, Sophia Hapgood, Colonel
George "Mac" McHale, and a young man who goes by the name
of "Short Round." [Our Chinese associates will note that Mr.
"Round" has included Chinese inscriptions in this journal,
which we've loosely translated as, "I like taking your money,
Dr. Jones." Intriguing.]

Known KGB agents with whom Dr. Jones interfaced:

████████████

Igor Barkov (captured)

█████████████

Elvira Kandinsky (deceased)

████████████████

Spalko (???)

We've taken the time to annotate worthy pages of the journal—
in English, for the benefit of our esteemed colleagues. Should
there be any further inquiries, please direct them to the
office of our Special Collections.

THE FEDERAL SECURITY SERVICE OF THE RUSSIAN FEDERATION

THE FEDERAL SECURITY SERVICE OF THE RUSSIAN FEDERATION

NOTE: Original cover to Dr. Jones's journal. Was damaged with age, and replaced with the current cover sometime around 1930, according to our experts. The ibis depicted is the symbol of Egyptian god Thoth, god of scribes.

FORM 21-A

April, 1908

I'm Indiana Jones. Actually, my real name is Henry, but that's my dad's name too so I like to be called Indiana. Dad just gave me this journal, because we left home because of Dad's job. He's a professor. Mother says I should be very happy about it and that if I am not, that I should write about it in this journal and not bring it up around Dad.

I think I am happy about it. We'll travel a lot, and I'll study with a tutor instead of going to school. So that sounds good to me!

THE FEDERAL SECURITY SERVICE OF THE RUSSIAN FEDERATION

NOTE: Ty Cobb was a controversial,
highly talented player. Regarded
the game as a war.

FORM 21-A

COBB, DETROIT

Ty Cobb, the best baseball player ever! That's one bad thing about leaving New Jersey, I guess. I haven't been able to listen to ball games on the radio.

We had a neighborhood baseball diamond, and I used to go there a lot. My favorite position is first base.

My dog, Indiana.
My best friend.

That's another bad
thing about moving.
We had to leave
Indiana. I'm going
to really miss him.

THE FEDERAL SECURITY SERVICE OF THE RUSSIAN FEDERATION

NOTE: Dr. Jones's crude depiction of
his animal indicates that Indiana was
an Alaskan Malamute. The creatures
weigh over 45.5 kg (100 lbs). They
are known to be highly intelligent,
stubborn, and extremely loyal.

FORM 21-A

Me and Dad in
New Jersey,
January 1908

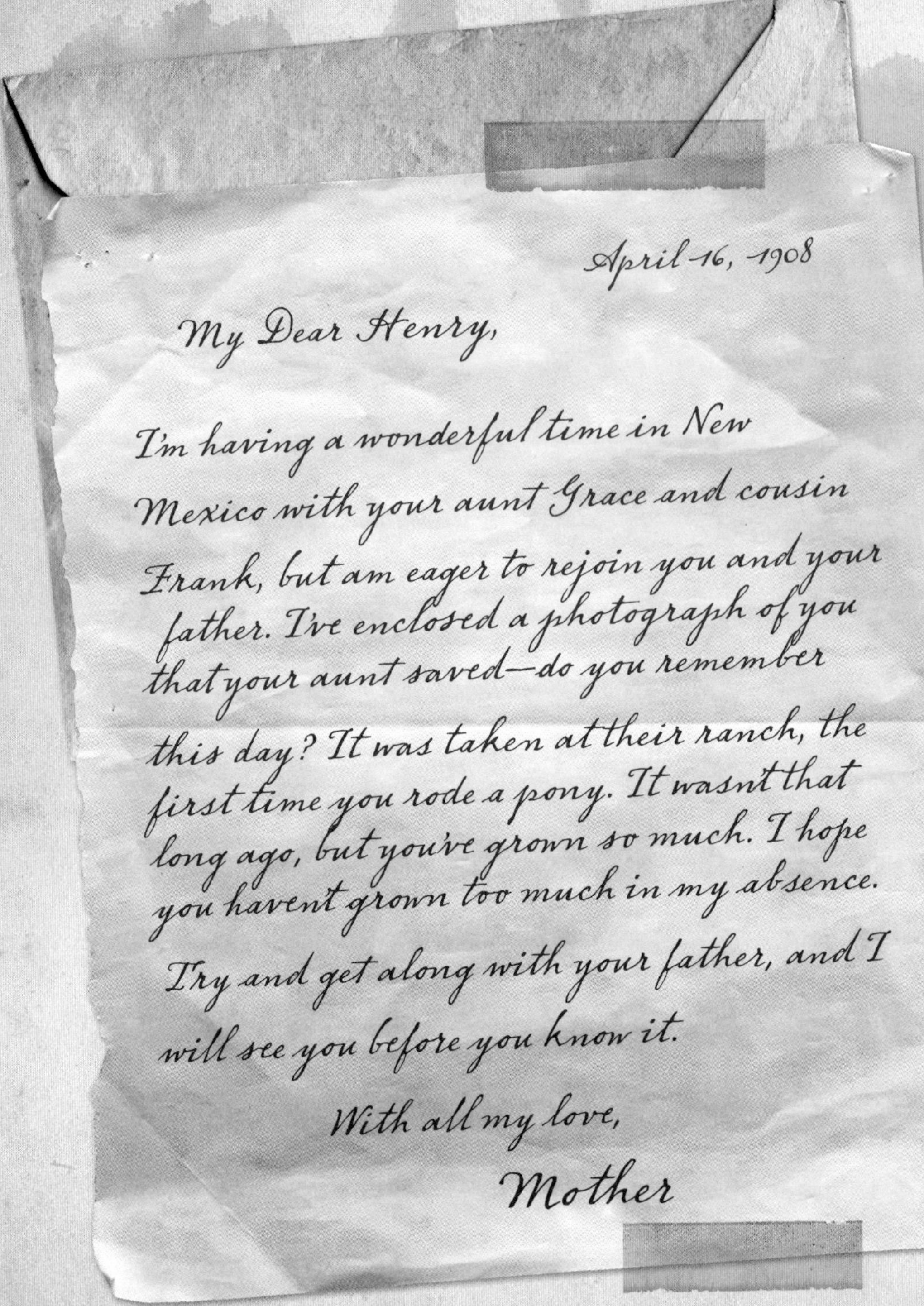

April 16, 1908

My Dear Henry,

I'm having a wonderful time in New Mexico with your aunt Grace and cousin Frank, but am eager to rejoin you and your father. I've enclosed a photograph of you that your aunt saved—do you remember this day? It was taken at their ranch, the first time you rode a pony. It wasn't that long ago, but you've grown so much. I hope you haven't grown too much in my absence.

Try and get along with your father, and I will see you before you know it.

With all my love,

Mother

Mother thinks riding this pony was a big deal for me. But it wasn't. It's just a little pony.

THE FEDERAL SECURITY SERVICE OF THE RUSSIAN FEDERATION

NOTE: Image dates from approximately 1905, or several years before the letter was written. The "cousin Frank" referred to here reappears in Indy's later years, which is also noted.

FORM 21-A

May 10, 1908

Dad's lecturing in Egypt, and it's been really fun here. I made a friend named Ned Lawrence (his real name is T.E., but I just call him Ned), and he took me on an ~~arciological~~ ~~archiological~~ archeological dig with a really nice man named Mr. Carter. It was great! He has a fun job.

THE FEDERAL SECURITY SERVICE OF THE RUSSIAN FEDERATION

NOTE: "Ned" is Thomas Edward Lawrence, a British researcher and lieutenant colonel in the Royal Air Force now known as "Lawrence of Arabia."

NOTE: "Mr. Carter" is Howard Carter, the British archeologist and Egyptologist best known for finding the tomb of King Tutankhamun in 1922.

FORM 21-A

me and Ned
Egypt - Spring 1908

May 9, 1908

Dear Henry,

No one knows where our respective journeys will take us. Let us make a pact to stay in touch. Letters can not come close to the adventures we've had together, but they are all we've got. You are an extraordinary young man, Henry. Keep learning about the world, and you will do well.

Your friend,
Ned

This is a sketch of the jackal. During the dig, someone took off with it, because it has ~~valueable~~ valuable jewels in the eyes. I'm going to get it back one day!

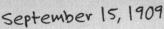

September 15, 1909

Right now I'm on a safari in British East Africa, in a place called Kirinyaga. Here's some of the things I've seen, and a picture of me with our leader, President Roosevelt, but he's not our President anymore!

I saw three giraffe in a clump of trees. They look to be very frendly and seem to be watching me.

This is the camp that we set up in Kirinyaga. The natives are very frendly and helpful. Roosevelt does his weight training near the camp. Mrs. Seymour laughs at all the noises and grunts that he makes very noiselly.

This gazelle is a dama gazelle (Gazella dama ruficollis) is what they told me he is properly called.

His horns are black and ridged. His fur looks very soft and has many colors, mostly browns and white.

The women of the village spend a lot of time with their children but also help gather food and even hunt sometimes.

There are many gazelles and other animals on the plains that run together in herds. They live together like a big family.

The village dog. He is a very good guard dog

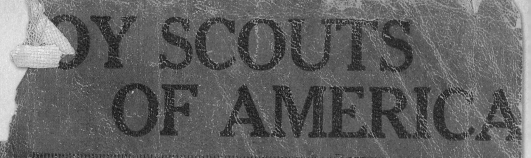
Life Scout

The life scout badge will be given to all first-class scouts who have qualified for the following five-merit badges: first aid, athletics, life-saving, personal health, and public health.

Star Scout

The star scout badge will be given to the first-class scout who has qualified for ten merit badges. The ten include the list of badges under life scout.

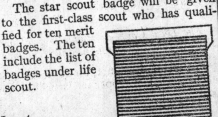

Eagle Scout

Any first-class scout qualifying for twenty-one merit badges will be entitled to wear the highest scout merit badge. This is an eagle's head in silver, and represents the all-round perfect scout.

June 8, 1912

It's been a long time since I've written. It's been a busy few years. Mother got sick, and died.
I don't really want to write about that, though.

TO THE MEMORY OF

ANNA MARY JONES

Died- March 3, 1912, Aged- 33 years

Dad and I moved to Utah. Here's a picture of our house. It's been okay here, it's nice to be in a new place, but it's very different now that it's just the two of us. I joined a new club called the Boy Scouts, and have met some interesting people. I like it out here. And I get to be with Indiana again!

Me and Dad, taken just when we moved to Utah.

August 1, 1912

Mr. Havelock from my troop is planning an overnight in Arches National Park. Which is swell. So Utah's all right. There are some amazing places to go digging for old arrowheads and artifacts, what with the Indians who used to live here and all. It's pretty hot, which I think has been hard for Indiana to get used to. I think he misses Mother, too.

Dad's in his study again. Looking at those same old sketches and maps. I think he's obsessed. We don't talk much, but we never did I guess. I just didn't notice it as much before. Now it's just the two of us and Indiana, only Dad's not even really here. But it's not worth spending time thinking about. I've got an overnight to get ready for!

THE FEDERAL SECURITY SERVICE OF THE RUSSIAN FEDERATION

NOTE: All indications are that the "same old sketches and maps" in which Dr. Jones the senior is interested pertain to his well-known, lifelong study of and search for the Holy Grail.

FORM 21-A

Packing List:

hat
uniform—can't forget neckerchiefs this time!
canteen
rucksack
journal

August 5, 1912

I was only able to look at the cross for a little while.

This drawing is from memory. It was gold with three or four pearls on each end.

There was some coloring on the edges (a dark blue, I think)

The Cross of Coronado...and all I have to show for all this is a cut on my chin! (and an old brown hat!)

The cross had a loop at the top and a heavy gold chain. On the back were words in Latin but I didn't have time to read them.

This is a sketch of the man who got the Cross, although then he handed it to someone else. Is he some sort of adventure-seeker for hire? Kind of weird; Dad wouldn't like it ...

- Black leather coat
- Brown eyes, brown hair, maybe 6'0
- Khaki pants
- Brown safari hat
  (NOTE: now in my possession)
- Scar on left cheek, about three inches long and sloped downward
- "You lost today kid, but you don't have to like it."

You're right. I don't.

Fell into a pit of snakes on the Dunn and Duffy Circus car. Long story. Met a lion, too, but it's the snakes that stay with you.

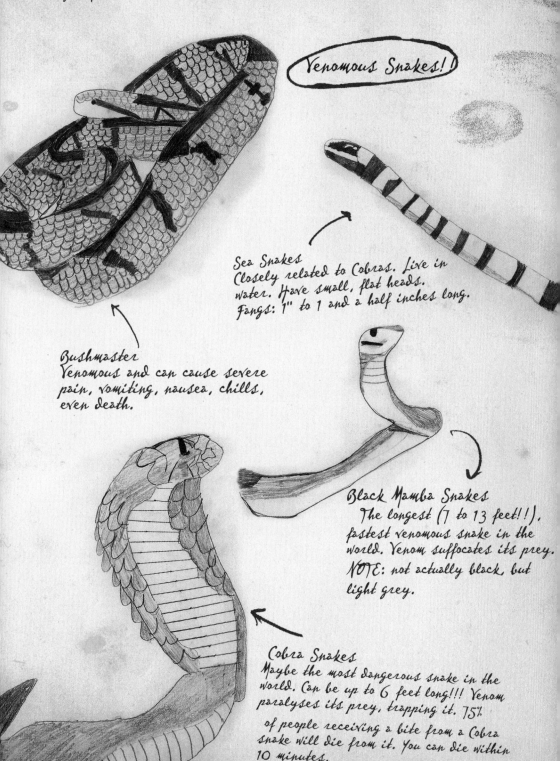

Venomous Snakes!!

Sea Snakes
Closely related to Cobras. Live in water. Have small, flat heads. Fangs: 1" to 1 and a half inches long.

Bushmaster
Venomous and can cause severe pain, vomiting, nausea, chills, even death.

Black Mamba Snakes
The longest (7 to 13 feet!!), fastest venomous snake in the world. Venom suffocates its prey. NOTE: not actually black, but light grey.

Cobra Snakes
Maybe the most dangerous snake in the world. Can be up to 6 feet long!!! Venom paralyses its prey, trapping it. 75% of people receiving a bite from a Cobra snake will die from it. You can die within 10 minutes.

March 9, 1916

Indiana Jones
c/o Frank Jones
10 La Placencia
Albuquerque, NM

Dear Indy,

I hope you're having a good time in New
Mexico with Frank and your aunt. Our
trip's going okay, but it would've been more
fun with you along. We didn't get to talk
much before you left, but I want you to
know I've definitely sensed your impatience
lately. I know you want to get out of
school, out of town, get some space from
your dad. You know, you can tell me things
like that. And you can tell me things you're
afraid will disappoint me, like that you
wouldn't be coming on spring break with
me. I can take it—it's only two weeks,
after all. I just wish you'd told me
earlier. Anyway, I think we've got a good
thing going and I just don't want anything
to come between us. I miss you.

Nancy ♡

March 15, 1916

I came out West on a trip with Dad, but I'm not going home. I'm in Mexico now, but I'm not staying here either. I joined up with Pancho Villa, but it's not really making sense for me to stay. I met a Belgian, Remy, and I think we're going to help fight a war that makes sense, in Europe. I got a letter from Ned, and he's fighting and thinks we can win.

Dear Dad,
I know this isn't what you would've expected of me. But I'm not sure you can really understand what's happening in Mexico, what the Revolution is all about, and why I feel I have to stay. Sometimes life takes us somewhere we ourselves don't expect, "the best laid schemes of mice and men . . ."

Dear Dad,
I've joined the Mexican Revolution. Sorry about high school. Take care of Indiana for me.

Your son,
Henry

There's just one thing I need to do before I leave Mexico— recover the jackal Ned and I saw stolen in Egypt! I've seen the man who has it! So I should have it soon, then I'm going to give it to a museum, where it belongs.

POBLACHT NA H EIREANN.

THE PROVISIONAL GOVERNMENT
OF THE
IRISH REPUBLIC
TO THE PEOPLE OF IRELAND

IRISHMEN AND IRISHWOMEN: In the name of God and of the dead generations from which she receives her old tradition of nationhood, Ireland, through us, summons her children to her flag and strikes for her freedom.

Having organised and trained her manhood through her secret revolutionary organisation, the Irish Republican Brotherhood, and through her open military organisations, the Irish Volunteers and the Irish Citizen Army, having patiently perfected her discipline, having resolutely waited for the right moment to reveal itself, she now seizes that moment, and, supported by her exiled children in America and by gallant allies in Europe, but relying in the first on her own strength, she strikes in full confidence of victory.

We declare the right of the people of Ireland to the ownership of Ireland, and to the unfettered control of Irish destinies, to be sovereign and indefeasible. The long usurpation of that right by a foreign people and government has not extinguished the right, nor can it ever be extinguished except by the destruction of the Irish people. In every generation the Irish people have asserted their right to national freedom and sovereignty; six times during the last three hundred years they have asserted it in arms. Standing on that fundamental right and again asserting it in arms in the face of the world, we hereby proclaim the Irish Republic as a Sovereign Independent State, and we pledge our lives and the lives of our comrades-in-arms to the cause of its freedom, of its welfare, and of its exaltation among the nations.

The Irish Republic is entitled to, and hereby claims, the allegiance of every Irishman and Irishwoman. The Republic guarantees religious and civil liberty, equal rights and equal opportunities to all its citizens, and declares its resolve to pursue the happiness and prosperity of the whole nation and all of its parts, cherishing all of the children of the nation equally and oblivious of the differences carefully fostered by an alien government, which have divided a minority from the majority in the past.

Until our arms have brought the opportune moment for the establishment of a permanent National, representative of the whole people of Ireland and elected by the suffrages of all her men and women, the Provisional Government, hereby constituted, will administer the civil and military affairs of the Republic in trust for the people.

We place the cause of the Irish Republic under the protection of the Most High God. Whose blessing we invoke upon our arms, and we pray that no one who serves that cause will dishonour it by cowardice, in humanity, or rapine. In this supreme hour the Irish nation must, by its valour and discipline and by the readiness of its children to sacrifice themselves for the common good, prove itself worthy of the august destiny to which it is called.

Signed on Behalf of the Provisional Government.

THOMAS J. CLARKE,

SEAN Mac DIARMADA, THOMAS MacDONAGH,

P. H. PEARSE, EAMONN CEANNT,

JAMES CONNOLLY, JOSEPH PLUNKETT

April 27, 1916

It's an odd time to be in England. Remy and I had to come here to enlist. There's been an attempted uprising in Ireland, though it doesn't look very promising for them.

Many here in England merely laugh about it, and have sent the military to take care of it. It seems like the whole world has gone mad. And I am in the middle of all the action!

It's unbelievable that I would otherwise have been in boring old Princeton, finishing school, working at the soda parlor. This is a much better education—I think even Dad might agree.

Perhaps not.

THE FEDERAL SECURITY SERVICE OF THE RUSSIAN FEDERATION

NOTE: Dr. Jones refers to the Easter Uprising of 1916, in which a group of men and women attempted to seize Dublin and eliminate British rule in Ireland. They failed.

FORM 21-A

Me and Remy in front of Big Ben in London, April 1916

August 1916

Fighting with Pancho Villa in Mexico was no preparation for the horrors of this war. Remy and I were sent to Flanders where all the officers in our troop were killed.

We were sent to join the French forces at the Somme to stop the German Army. War is indescribable. How anyone survives it is a miracle.

NOTHING is to be written on this side except the date and signature of the sender. Sentences not required may be erased. If anything else is added the post card will be destroyed.

I am quite well.

I have been admitted into hospital

{ sick } and am going on well,

{ wounded } and hope to be discharged soon,

I am being sent down to the base.

I have received your { letter dated / telegram " / parcel "

Letter follows at first opportunity.

I have received no letter from you

{ lately

{ for a long time

Signature only } Remy Baudur, W

Date 12 Sept 1918

[Postage must be prepaid on any letter or post card addressed to the sender of this card.]

THE FEDERAL SECURITY SERVICE OF THE RUSSIAN FEDERATION

NOTE: Records indicate that Dr. Jones went by the alias "Henri Defense" for the duration of the Great War. He ultimately received the rank of captain, and served for the Belgian army in France; East Africa; Petrograd, Russia; Prague; Beersheba; Romania; Northern Italy; and Istanbul. He seems to have held a range of jobs, from motorcycle courier, to translator, to positions in espionage and intelligence.

FORM 21-A

During the advance we were shot at with machine guns, gassed, even nearly burned alive by flame throwers. Remy was hurt, but judging from this telegram I just got, he is going to be okay. There was nothing I could do but fight. And kill.

Army Form C 213
(In books of 100.)
No. of Message...............

		Sent, or sent out.	Office Stamp.

Prefix S.M. Code 0820 Words 62

Received from 2E.I. By Rendon T.

Service Instructions YT

Sent, or sent out.
At................m.
To..................
By..................

Office Stamp.
KRK
11/11/18

Handed in at 20th Divn Office 0820 m. Received 0840 m.

TO All Bns.

*Sender's Number.	Day of Month.	**In reply to Number.	
GB914	11th		AAA

Following from 17th Corps staned 0635 Hostilities will cease 1100 Hours today Nov 11th aaa Troops will stand fast on line reached at that hour which will be reported by wire to Corps HQ aaa Defensive precautions will be maintained aaa There will be no intercourse of any description with the enemy

FROM 20th Divn
PLACE & TIME 0730

* This line except AAA should be entered ** not required.

November 20, 1918
After two of the longest years of my life, it
seems to be over. Not much time to write lately...
and events too terrible to write about.

We just learned of a cease-fire in the war, and I
have this telegram to prove it. I plan to keep it with me
always as a reminder of just how bad it was for a while.

Nov. 22, 1918

Remy and I found a map on a corporal shot in no mans land that may lead us to the "Eye of the Peacock"

On the map was written in English a reference to the tomb of Lycomedes. We are sailing to Alexandria to begin our quest.

This golden peacock was owned by Alexander the Great. Its eyes were 140 karat diamonds

THE FEDERAL SECURITY SERVICE OF THE RUSSIAN FEDERATION

NOTE: Our research shows that the peacock in question was not of value. Rather, it was only the jeweled eyes that Dr. Jones sought. For years, it seems.

NOTE: Lycomedes is a character in Greek mythology. He was the King of Scyros during the Trojan War.

FORM 21-A

Nov. 29, 1918

From the tomb. Note that the rider on horseback is Alexander the Great. Also note, he's in front of the <u>middle</u> mountain.
Could be important...

ΠΟΛΕΙΤΑΡΧΟΥΝΩ
Ν·ΣΩΣΑΙΤΑΤΡΟΥΤΧ
ΡΑΥΣΤΩΜΕΔΚΑΓΔΙ
ΓΕΜΟΛΥΕΡΛΓΝΩ
ΔΗΜΤΡΟΙΣΑΜΥΓ
———
ΛΥΥΓΟΔΟΜΑ

Translation: "The dragon is the key to your dreams" ?

~~Yale~~ *rejected*

~~Northwestern~~ *rejected!*

U Chicago *haven't heard yet*

Penn State *good sociolinguistics program*

~~Harvard~~ *rejected*

Washington

NYU *applied late...*

Cornell

MIT *theoretical linguistics*

~~U Mass, Amherst~~ *no arch program...*

University of Chicago   Fall 1920
Declared Major: Linguistics   Class Schedule

1. Anth 37802 Syntax Intermediate
   3 credits   M, W 8:20 a.m.

2. Ling 20800 Historical Linguistics
   3 credits   M, W 11:00 a.m.

3. Bio 20181 Biology Intro/Genetics
   3 credits   T, Th 1:25 p.m.

4. Bio 20181 Bio Intro Lab
   1 credit   Th 4:30 p.m.

5. Intro to Russian Civilization
   3 credits   T, Th 9:40 a.m.

Junior:
I don't understand this ridiculous notion to go to university for archeology. Why don't you use your brain and get a real education? Linguistics, history... Anything with a little substance. You're smarter than this, boy.

-Dr. Henry Jones

Delphi, Greece—1922

eastern pediment

Dr. Belecamus, my archeology professor, wanted me to accompany her on this dig as an ancient Greek linguist. We are attempting to decipher an unknown Greek script called Liniu B. We found a crevice that I was lowered into, because it held a tablet we couldn't extricate. I wrote down the markings on the tablet, which were:

We have our work cut out for us!

June 27, 1925

My Dear Indiana,

I trust you are doing well and I hope this letter and journal comes as a pleasant surprise to you. It seems that myth does have a basis in truth. My life's obsession for a lost object of history has led me to believe I may be very close to finding an item of the greatest archeological significance-the Ark of the Covenant.

However, I have fallen victim to the great scourge of this academic discipline: the pain of finding funds. So, I extend my begging bowl and kindly request your help on this last expedition before returning you to your teaching obligations at Marshall College. I am certain your fresh insight will undoubtedly help to bring an end to years of fruitless excavations. My journal should familiarize you with the most recent findings.

Should you agree, bear in mind that the route is a devious one, which will take you from the United States through San Francisco to Hong Kong, Shanghai, Kathmandu and further on to the Nepalese region of Patan.

Looking forward to hopefully seeing you again my dear friend,

Yours Faithfully,

Abner

THE FEDERAL SECURITY SERVICE OF THE RUSSIAN FEDERATION

NOTE: "Abner" is the aforementioned Abner Ravenwood, onetime archeology professor at the University of Chicago, mentor to Dr. Jones, and known scholar of the Ark of the Covenant. Ravenwood had one child: a daughter named Marion, also an acquaintance of Dr. Jones.

FORM 21-A

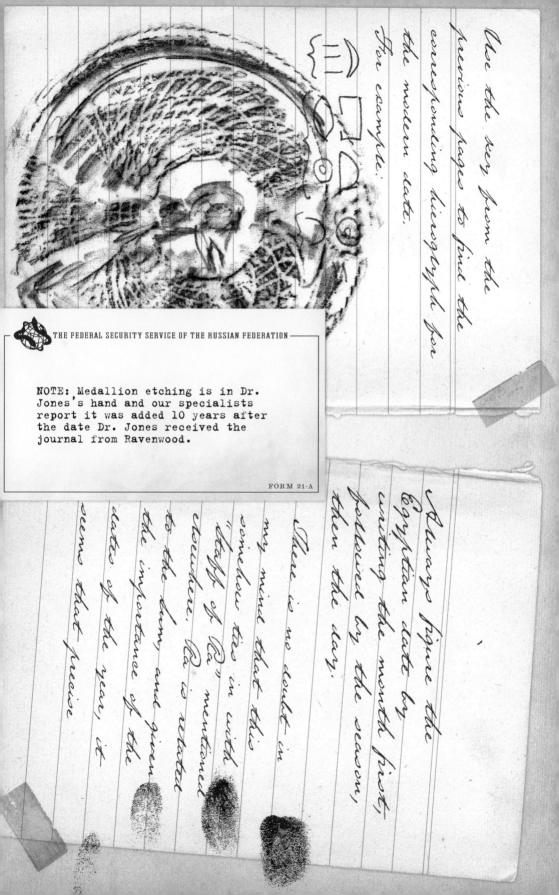

Use the key from the previous pages to find the corresponding hieroglyph for the modern date. For example:

Always figure the Egyptian date by writing the month first, followed by the season, then the day.

There is no doubt in my mind that this somehow ties in with "Staff of Ra" mentioned elsewhere. Ra is related to the Sun and given the importance of the dates of the year, it seems that precise

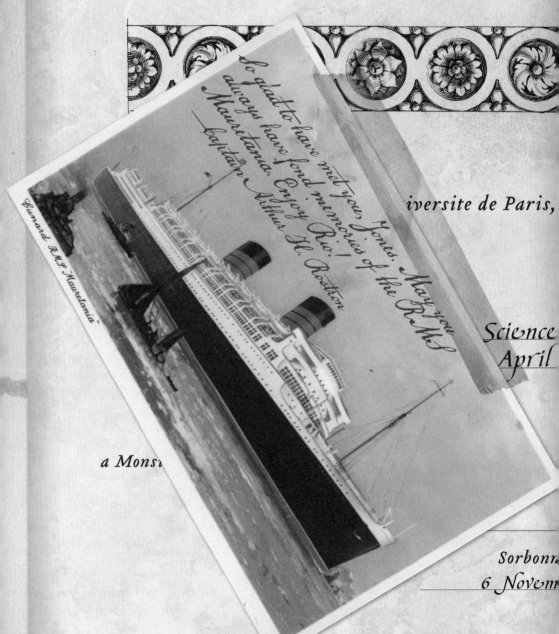

iversite de Paris,

Science
April

a Monsi

Sorbonn
6 Novem

Cunard R.M.S. "Mauretania"

So glad to have met you, Jones. May you
always have fond memories of the R.M.S.
Mauretania. Enjoy Rio!
Captain Arthur H. Rostron

March 1926
Tikal, Guatemala

Deidre and I
discovered this
Maya funerary
mask of the bat
god Camazotz

Next stop: Rio de Janeiro

May 1933

It looks like I'm moving back to Princeton, after all these years.
I've been offered a job teaching in the university's archeology department, which is a very esteemed one. They were pleased with my linguistics background, so I guess I owe a debt of thanks to Dad for that.

...forces as well ...Fuhrer of the ...o whom every ...vidual in the ...pledged un- ...ence.

...S TO POWER

...32 elections, the ...ncreased their ...Reichstag to 230 ...of them in the ...tions. Radical ...o seize power, ...isted that he ...power legally ...would accept ...than the ...The internal ...n, meanwhile, ...ble and many ...evolted by the ...ghting of the ...n the summer ...z von Papen ...st bulwark of ...cy, the federal ..., by charging ...d not maintain ...In the process, ...me the Reich ...for Prussia, ...of all of ...es and a police ...which Hitler ...

GRAVE ROBBER OR ARCHEOLOGIST?

Dr. Indiana Jones Wanted By Honduran Government

SAN PABLO, Friday, March 24 - Though details are sketchy, it is clear that the government of British Honduras has issued a warrant of arrest for American archeologist Dr. Indiana Jones of Princeton University. According to the official report, Dr. Jones illegally removed a precious artifact from a sacred well inside the ancient city of Cozan. Officials accuse him of stealing a large crystal quartz artifact which is now for sale on the "black market." Dr. Jim Awe, the Director of Antiquities, refused to comment on the exact nature of the missing artifact.

Dr. Jones is also wanted as a suspect in the disappearance of an Italian tourist along with Leonardo Sarducci, an associate of the missing man.

Princeton chairman Harold Gruber stated that the University agent is looking into the charges and that he would certainly not defend Jones' "grave robbing" if the rumors prove to be true.+

Commis... gaining... Prussia... force o... later a... Party.

In Con...

On M... Reichstag... house,... forces... Stormtroo... of the Cer... for Hitl... necessary... to pass a... this they... him the... craved. F... power wi... and ignor... opposing... destroyed... selves.... liquidated... were arre... has, in F... the state... when Hi... also bec... chief of th... as Presid... German... officer a... armed...

They also seemed to be supportive of the traveling necessary to my research. We'll see how long <u>that</u> lasts.

Update, India: Meeting at the Club Obi Wan
was not successful.

As for the diamond, here's a quick
sketch from memory... I only got one
good look at it before, let's see, I was
poisoned, shot at, sabotaged, crash-
landed, and rode down the mountain on
a life raft; not bad for a day's work

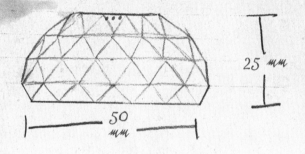

25 mm

50
mm

Dear Remy,

I'm not even sure if I should send you this note, and
perhaps I won't... maybe you'd rather not know any of
this. I have good news and bad news. I found the
Peacock's Eye! In China, if you can believe it. And
then it flew out of my grasp again. But I have a good
lead on where to look next...

CLUB OBI WAN

美
國
著
名
藝
人
每
晚
於
澳

比
灣
俱
樂
部
隆
重
登
場

特
戚
利
史
考

WILLIE SCOTT
Famous American Entertainer

CLUB OBI WAN

I could go to New Delhi and back in the
time it probably took her to do her hair...

For Indy —
my greatest fan!
xoxo,
Willie

Instruction Manual

for

Ford Trimotor

TO-DO LIST:

1. Reclaim the Peacock's Eye
2. Return library books/pay fines
3. Send invoice to Brody for artifact recovery
4. Finish course evaluations
5. Learn how to fly plane

Mayapore Village, December 1935

Arrived here after the strangest crash landing
I've had. And I've had some.

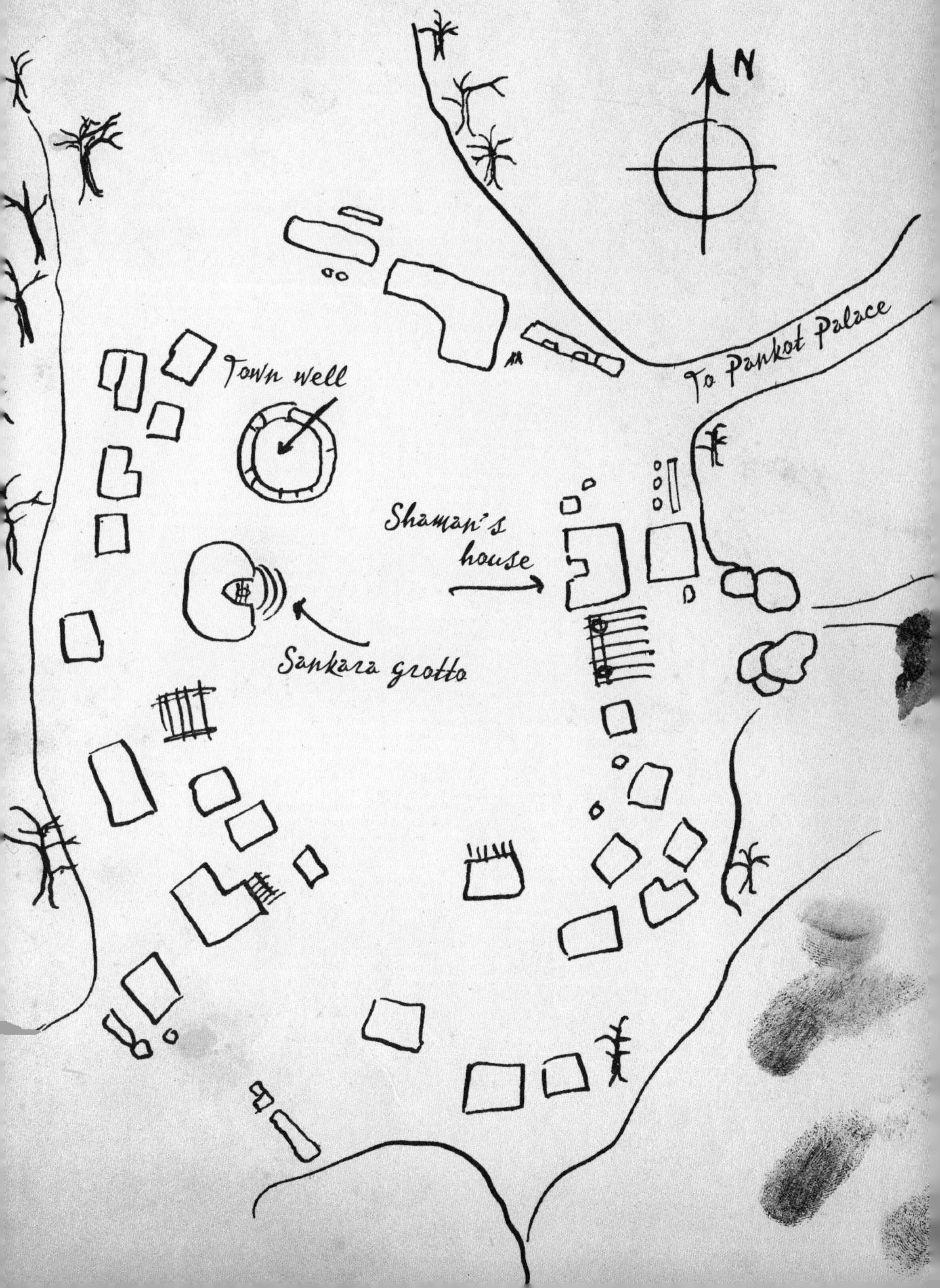

N

Town well

To Pankot Palace

**Shaman's
house** →

← **Sankara grotto**

Given to me by a village boy, who'd escaped. All
the children of this village were kidnapped, and
I'm going to figure out where they are.

The village used to have a sankara stone, which they say has been taken.
As a result they also say their village is cursed.

"Feasting" in the Shaman's hut. It seems like Willie decided to take photos just when it would offend our hosts the most.

NOTE: Get the kid his own hat for Chinese New Year.

The Sankara Stones (or Sivalinga) represent the power of the god Shiva.

The three carved lines on the stones represent the levels of the universe in Hindu cosmology.

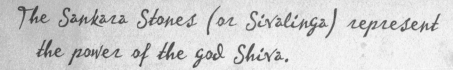

THE FEDERAL SECURITY SERVICE OF THE RUSSIAN FEDERATION

NOTE: Hindus believe the universe was birthed by creator Brahma, maintained by Vishnu, god of presence, and destroyed by Shiva, god of destruction—only to begin again.

FORM 21-A

Many villages have their own lingam, usually a naturally occurring stone, polished smooth by a sacred river. Though sometimes they are made of metal, precious gems, crystal, wood, or earth.

The Sankara Stones are of the former class, very smooth with a flattened base.

The legend of Sankara says there are diamonds inside the stones which, when brought
together, glow. This recounts the legend of the
fiery pillar that confounded the gods Brahma and
Vishnu, and from which emerged Shiva himself.

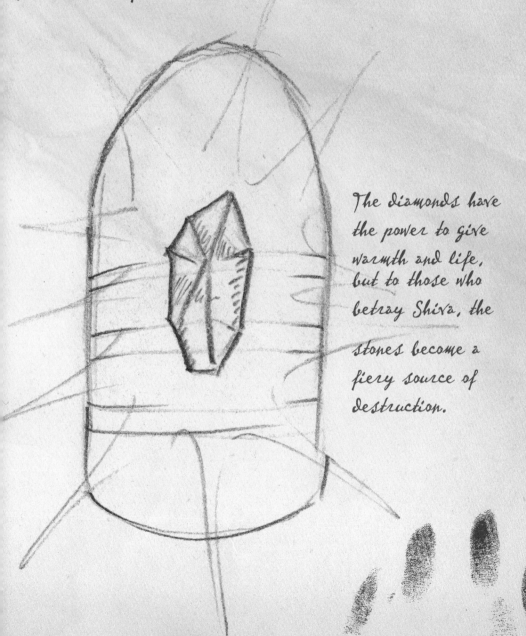

The diamonds have
the power to give
warmth and life,
but to those who
betray Shiva, the

stones become a
fiery source of
destruction.

Shaman.
Short Round thinks
he's 110. He might be
right this time...
I don't think he
appreciated having his
picture taken, but
Willie didn't ask.

Mayapore
Village

Kali Statue

Pankot Palace

Kali
Statues

Campsite for
last night's stop

HA HA, DR. JONES!
YOU ARE SO BAD AT POKER.
NO WONDER
I BEAT YOU.

你是個好人。
我很想和你打牌，
好想念從你那贏錢的日子啊。
哈哈。

Pankot Palace - Dec. 1935

According to Captain Blumburtt, the site of the palace of Pankot was once the center of activity for the Thuggee cult, featuring a large temple of Kali

The current Maharajah of Pankot is the young Zalim Singh

The Thuggee cult was officially and violently suppressed in 1828, which included the destruction of this temple. Colonialism for better and for worse...

The current palace was built over its remains, completed in 1839.

During the Mutiny of 1857, it served as a base of operations for the Indian rebels. By 1858, the Crown had established the India Office, placing Pankot and its Maharajah under the rule of Great Britain.

 THE FEDERAL SECURITY SERVICE OF THE RUSSIAN FEDERATION

NOTE: Dr. Jones is referring to the
Sepoy Mutiny of 1857 and 1858, in which
Indian troops unsuccessfully rebelled
against British Empire colonial rule.

FORM 21-A

THE ILLUSTRATED WORLD NEWS

No. 374 - Vol. XIV.]   FOR THE WEEK ENDING SATURDAY, JUNE 13, 1857.   [Sixpence.

DEADLY HINDOO ASSASSINS

British officials are working tirelessly to eliminate a grave threat continuing to disrupt the British Empire and its subjects in India. Thuggee (Thugs), gangs of ritualistic assassins, continue to haunt south Asia. They travel throughout India in highly organized gangs of various sizes. Nearly impossible to track, these deathly silent killers will stalk their victims for an extended period of time, sometimes even in their very company, in order to eventually strangle them when inspiration strikes. Thugs view strangulation as art. The body is then mutilated and offered as a sacrifice to the Hindu goddess Kali.

Each moment of the process, from choosing victims through murder and sacrificial offering, is purportedly dictated by Kali via a series of complex signs. Those that do not actively participate in the murders, such as the elderly or incapacitated, play logistical roles such as spying, and cooking. Once the subject is chosen, each murder occurs in a nearly identical fashion.

The strangler never operates barehanded. Whether with a handkerchief, wire, or rope, Thug assassins always use some sort of noose, earning them the Sanskrit title *phansigars*, which roughly translates to noose operators. In honor of this goddess of destruction, the body is then mutilated as part of a carefully scripted rite involving sugar and consecration of the weapon used in the defacement.

Generally the victim's head is brought to the goddess' altar. It is believed that Kali feasts on the blood of the murdered, and that she prefers males.

All of this is done in honor of Kali, and in the hope of keeping her wrath at bay for the millennium. The murderers feel no guilt. In fact, they firmly believe themselves to be fulfilling a deeply religious duty.

Although their origin connects them to early Mohammaden tribes, and Kali is a recognized Hindu goddess, this violent sect is no longer accepted as part of the peaceful Islam religion. However, since the 13th century, under the umbrella of religion, the cult assassins were recognized as a legitimate organization that even paid taxes. Luckily Captain Sleeman stood up in 1828, under the leadership of Lord William Bentinck, and organized against the rampant murders. After forming a committee of dedicated agents, and working with native Indian states, Sleeman oversaw the capture of thousands of Thugs. Over 400 were subsequently hanged.

Sleeman and his crew have succeeded admirably throughout the last twenty years in diminishing the threat. However, with their talent for extreme confidentiality, the group still exists in small numbers. At least 300 deaths have been attributed to Thugs. The Queen's agents continue to pursue this terrible horde to this day.

POISONER.   NUJEEB IN DISGUISE.   POISONER.   THUG. POISONER. THUG.   NUJEEB POLICEMAN.

HINDOO THUGS AND POISONERS. - FROM A DRAWING BY MR. W. CARPENTER.

THE GUARDIAN OF TRADITION DINNER

Gently Roasted vanAhira

Large wild boar garnished with
tender, suckling offspring

Coiled Wrigglies ("Snake Surprise")

Fresh live baby eels stuffed in
a moist boa constrictor shell

Cristpy Coleoptera

Fresh beetles, still in the shell, bursting
with meltingly delectable innards

Soup of the Head

Delicacies of boiled sheep head
floating in salty broth

Primate Parfait

Chilled, soft monkey brains,
served in monkey heads

Full of fiber, very satisfying.
Got Willie an apple.

DR. JONES IS A
LIAR!! IT WAS
GROSS

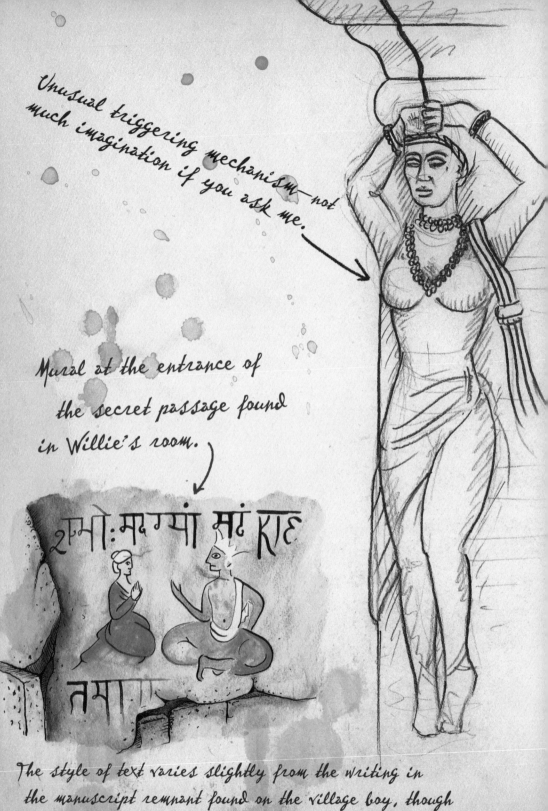

Unusual triggering mechanism—not much imagination if you ask me.

Mural at the entrance of the secret passage found in Willie's room.

शम्भो: मदग्यां सतां काह

तसा

The style of text varies slightly from the writing in the manuscript remnant found on the village boy, though the meaning is the same.

stick creature
note: should look this up

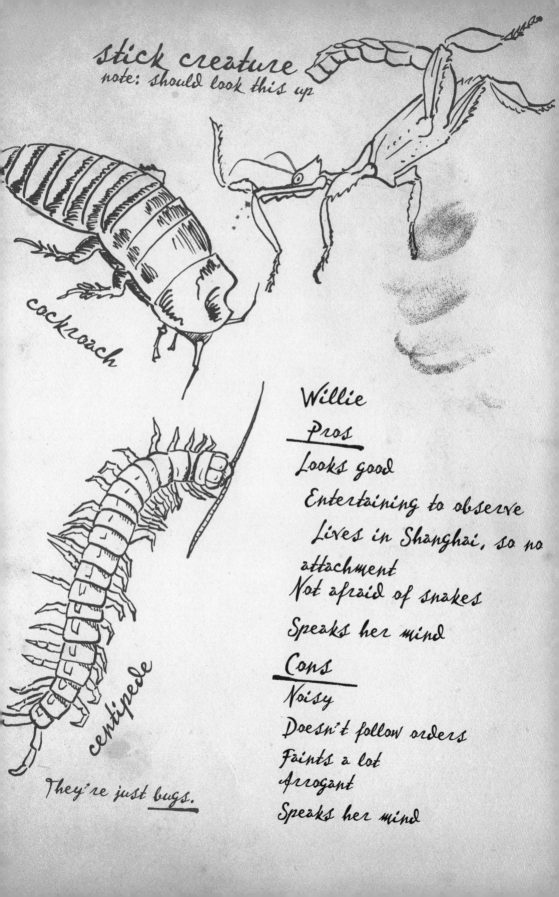

cockroach

centipede

They're just bugs.

Willie

Pros
Looks good
Entertaining to observe
Lives in Shanghai, so no attachment
Not afraid of snakes
Speaks her mind

Cons
Noisy
Doesn't follow orders
Faints a lot
Arrogant
Speaks her mind

Sketch of a room I'd really rather not be in again.

Maybe I should go solo. The kid's great, but doesn't follow instructions like he should. He triggered something and the floor and ceiling closed in on us-and let's not forget the razor-sharp spikes.

Had to rely on Willie to get us out, which is another situation I'd rather not be in again.

The woman falls apart when she sees a little bug or two.

PAGANISM IN INDIA

In one of the most prevalent depictions of Kali, she appears during an ecstatic killing spree. With a bloody sword in one of her four hands, and a severed demon head in another, the goddess dances frenetically, entranced and overjoyed by the bloodbath. In an effort to stop her, her husband Shiva dives under her feet. As she realizes what she has done, she sticks out her tongue in shock.

Amongst the Hindu religions, worshipers approach Kali in many different ways. Some consider her a benevolent mother figure; others believe she eases the fear of death. Often, she is depicted as a bloodthirsty destroyer, but is still believed to bless those who worship her.

The Thuggee, recognized as a cult more than a religion, offer human sacrifices as a means to win her favor. It is possible that these worshipers call upon black magic, such as the voodoo practices prevalent in New Orleans. However, this theory remains debatable, as voodoo is virtually unheard of in India. Yet, similarities do arise between Louisiana's voodoo and Nkishi in Central Africa, so the possibility that the ritual spread to India exists.

Photostat of book found in the Burke J. Carter Library at Marshall College.

According to legend, the priest Sankara climbs mount Kalisa where he meets the god Shiva.

There the god gives him five sacred stones with magical properties. With these, he tells him to go forth and combat evil.

Sankara travelled throughout India defeating many philosophers and ascetics, converting them to the ways of Shiva. After his death, the stones were lost.

Scene of Thuggee ritual, in which the heart is taken out of the live victim's chest—by hand—and he is lowered into fire pit.

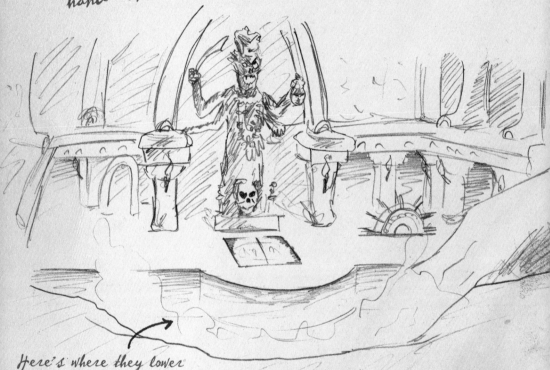

Here's where they lower their victims into pit.

When I return to school, need to research scientific, medical explanation for heart extraction. Unlike anything I've witnessed previously.

This chalice seems to have been made using a partially mummified human head with a gold "tongue" being used as its spout. →

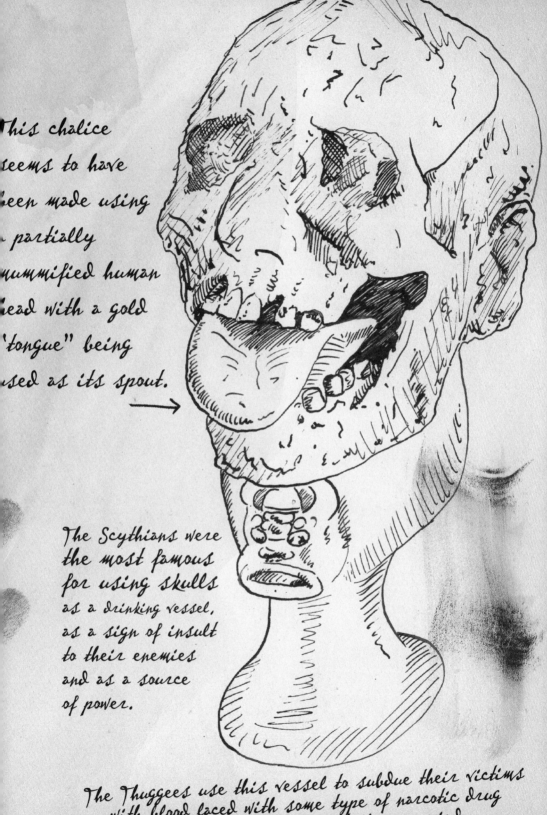

The Scythians were the most famous for using skulls as a drinking vessel, as a sign of insult to their enemies and as a source of power.

The Thuggees use this vessel to subdue their victims with blood laced with some type of narcotic drug that enables them to control your mind.

I ALWAYS SAY TO DR. JONES, YOU LISTEN ME, YOU LIVE LONGER. NEXT TIME HE WILL. I SAY TO HIM DON'T DRINK THE KALI BLOOD, WHICH MAKE HIM ACT CRAZY.

THEN THESE GUYS THEY TRY TO WHIP ME, BUT I DON'T CRY.

THEN THEY TAKE ME TO THE MINES, BUT I CHOP THROUGH MY CHAINS AND RUN OUT OF THERE.

GUYS WAS CHASING ME, KIDS WAS CHEERING ME, AND I GOT OUT AND BACK TO DR. JONES. BUT NEXT TIME DR. JONES NEED TO LISTEN TO ME SOONER.

Neem Leaf

given to me by the children of the
Mayapore Village

They call it
"Veppam"

Used throughout India as a medicinal, and
specifically in this region as a gift of
thanks due to the importance of the
Neem tree.

DR. JONES AND WILLIE, THEY SO HAPPY THIS DAY.

AND I FOUND MY BABY ELEPHANT!!!

These flowers were given
to me by a little girl
named Chataryna.

They seem to be a local variety of poppy.

Feb. 12, 1936

Dear Dr. Jones,

It was wonderful to hear from you. It goes without
saying that our stall in correspondence has gone
on far too long. Not to make pitiful excuses, but
I've been busier than ever with my class-load and
research duties, and frankly, when my past two
letters to you went unanswered, I figured I would let
you initiate contact. And so you have!

To answer your question, no, I'm afraid I've lost
touch with Dr. Ravenwood. As you know, after he left
the University we did continue our correspondence
for a time. But he is as poor at regular
correspondence as you are (forgive me), and soon
I gave it up. I have also heard he's somewhere in
Asia, and I've heard rumors from colleagues that he
and his daughter at one point were running a tavern
in Nepal. But I have no idea how to reach him. And
forgive me for saying so, but I'm not sure you
should try. If Dr. Ravenwood can't be counted on to
write even to me, I'm not sure contacting him would
be worth your time.

I do hope all is well at Marshall College. Every so
often I teach a graduate student who has studied
there previously, and all reports are excellent.

Yours truly,

Professor David Pierson

Cairo Museum
Boulak, Egypt.

February 1st, 1936

My Dear Indy,

    Peace be upon you, my old friend. I have recently been told about
your safe return to America after your aeroplane crash-landed in India. I
am so glad to hear that you are not dead.

    Cairo has changed much since you visited last year. There is a major
German dig taking place outside the city. They are hiring every digger they
can find though pay pennies only. I do not understand why the British are
allowing these Nazis to work so closely to our capital city. Surely trouble
will arise.

Your servant,

Sallah Mohammed Faisel el-Kahir

THE FEDERAL SECURITY SERVICE OF THE RUSSIAN FEDERATION

NOTE: "Sallah," a known longstanding
archeological acquaintance of Dr.
Jones. Father of many children,
lifelong resident of Cairo. Involved
in subversive activities. See relevant
file in Stasi file #79-1340-SMFK.

FORM 21-A

"Your Daily Source of Important News"

The Daily Chr

VOL. XCII. No. 21,345.

NEW YORK, MONDAY, JANUARY 6, 1936.

TENSIONS RISE AS NAZI

ROOSEVELT WARNS OF WAR

The Congressmen expecting a repeat of last year's highly optimistic Inaugural Address received a shock today. The President began his speech praising peace within the United States, and ended by speaking at length about his plans to both balance the budget and continue to aid those affected by the Depression. However, sandwiched between these predictable talking points, the President discussed foreign policy:

The temper and the purposes of the rulers of many of the great populations in Europe...have not pointed the way either to peace or to good-will among men...A point has been reached where the people of the Americas must take cognizance of growing ill-will, of marked trends toward aggression, of increasing armaments, of shortening tempers - a situation which has in it many of the elements that lead to the tragedy of general war.

Mr. Roosevelt never candidly mentions Hitler and his Nazis, but with Germany's recent rejection of Geneva and refusal

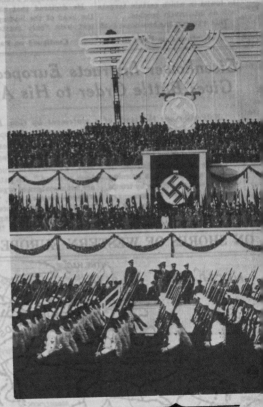

League of Nations High Commissio

James Grover McDonald announced his the position of League of Nations High C Refugees from Germany at London's Nemesi lengthy written statement, he sites the ref nations to address the "unspeakable abus Germany.

A resignation with this fervor seems to sig realization of Hitler's dangerous goals. Read Führer's words following the enactment o Law" in March, "The Nazi party has be McDonald's view suggests there is truth to Great Powers are ignoring the rise of the Naz

MORNING EDITION

Partly cloudy with showers;
moderate to fresh winds.

THREE CENTS

AIN POWER

Hitler's Assertions

th
F
F
t

Cher Jones:

I understand we have yet another object of mutual interest in South America. I do so enjoy these holidays with you, bien sûr. I hear Forrestal is also joining us, so the reunion will be complete. In fact, I have learned that his arrival predates either of ours, so he is sure to have scouted out the fairest destinations.

Avec mes meilleurs regards,
René Belloq

Lava
Desp
and fierce batt
Deputies, Laval
resign.

gns

In addition, it
from Hitler has offere
for an air pact with
in his admitting no
erful This strategic me
g in effort by the N
nued Britain and Fra
ll the the British are
bling long awaited soccer victory over
tate." New Zealand tonight, however
at the a darker competition could be
lurking beneath the surface.

THE FEDERAL SECURITY SERVICE OF THE RUSSIAN FEDERATION

NOTE: René Belloq, esteemed French
archeologist and known rival of Dr.
Jones's. See file KG-T-135 and file
acquired from the Sureté.

FORM 21-A

PROFESSOR EVALUATION

Marshall College

Course: ARCH, Spring 1936

Professor: DR. HENRY JONES, JR.

Evaluator: DR. CHARLES KENNEDY

Signature: *Charles Kennedy*

Date: April 12, 1936

Student Support Despite the unorthodox teaching methods of Dr. Jones, students are quite enthusiastic about attending his courses. This is especially true among the female student body; however, Jones does not let his popularity in this area affect his overall professionalism. Jones's extensive traveling, of course, prevents him from assisting students on their term papers throughout the semester. The department accepts this with the understanding that he must provide another professor or assistant to answer questions in his absence.

Exams Dr. Jones's exams are thorough and quite detailed. He challenges his students not only to be knowledgeable of the processes, but also to understand the meaning behind each method. Like any good scientist, he leaves no stone unturned. I would like to see Jones grade his exams in a timelier manner, though, as students are often very eager to see their scores. Travel is important to research, but allowing students time to use their exams to make progress is also a large goal of the department's.

Research Dr. Jones is very zealous in his research, preferring the hands-on approach. The public recognition resulting from his findings has benefited the university, although it must be understood that we must take into consideration negative publicity as well.

Susan Ryan

Archeology 101, Term Paper, 1936

Archeological Artifacts and Folklore

The problem of looting of historically important archeological territories and its artifacts is an old one. To help, archeologists must make sure cultural property and significant sites are known and monitored. Archeologists need to put together exacting inventories of artifacts for law enforcement agencies, and promptly notify law enforcement of any theft or illicit activity.

An excellent example of this is what happened in England with the Hazleton Long Barrows. Though everyone knew it was true that there were burial chambers there, there was a story that there was a golden coffin, too. So what happened? People tried to find them, by digging holes. All this meant was devastation of the site. But they had good reasons for digging where they did, as folklore also

Doesn't work this way, kid.

No— never marks the spot.

Reminder: Must get this paper back to Ms. Ryan for revisions. Might have to ask review board for extension in filing grades, since this is late.

Susan: Revisions due 5/15

I'm en route to South America, to bring back an artifact for Marcus. I'll probably run into Forrestal and Bellog. Not sure if I'd rather be first or have them be first.

— Look for this at entrance of Chachapoyan Temple

Need to contact Jock Lindsay once I get there. I have some good leads on porters to hire. Shd. be interesting.

SCHEDULE OF FARES
See Special Folder for Sailings

SOUTH AMERICA

FORTNIGHTLY SAILINGS

GRACE LINE

One Way and Round Trip Fares Between

NEW YORK
PANAMA CANAL
COLOMBIA
ECUADOR
PERU
CHILE
HAVANA ~ Northbound

Finest, Fastest Service

GRACE LINE
10 Hanover Sq. & New York
Phone: BEekman 3-9200

From Bandelier's collection in New Mexico

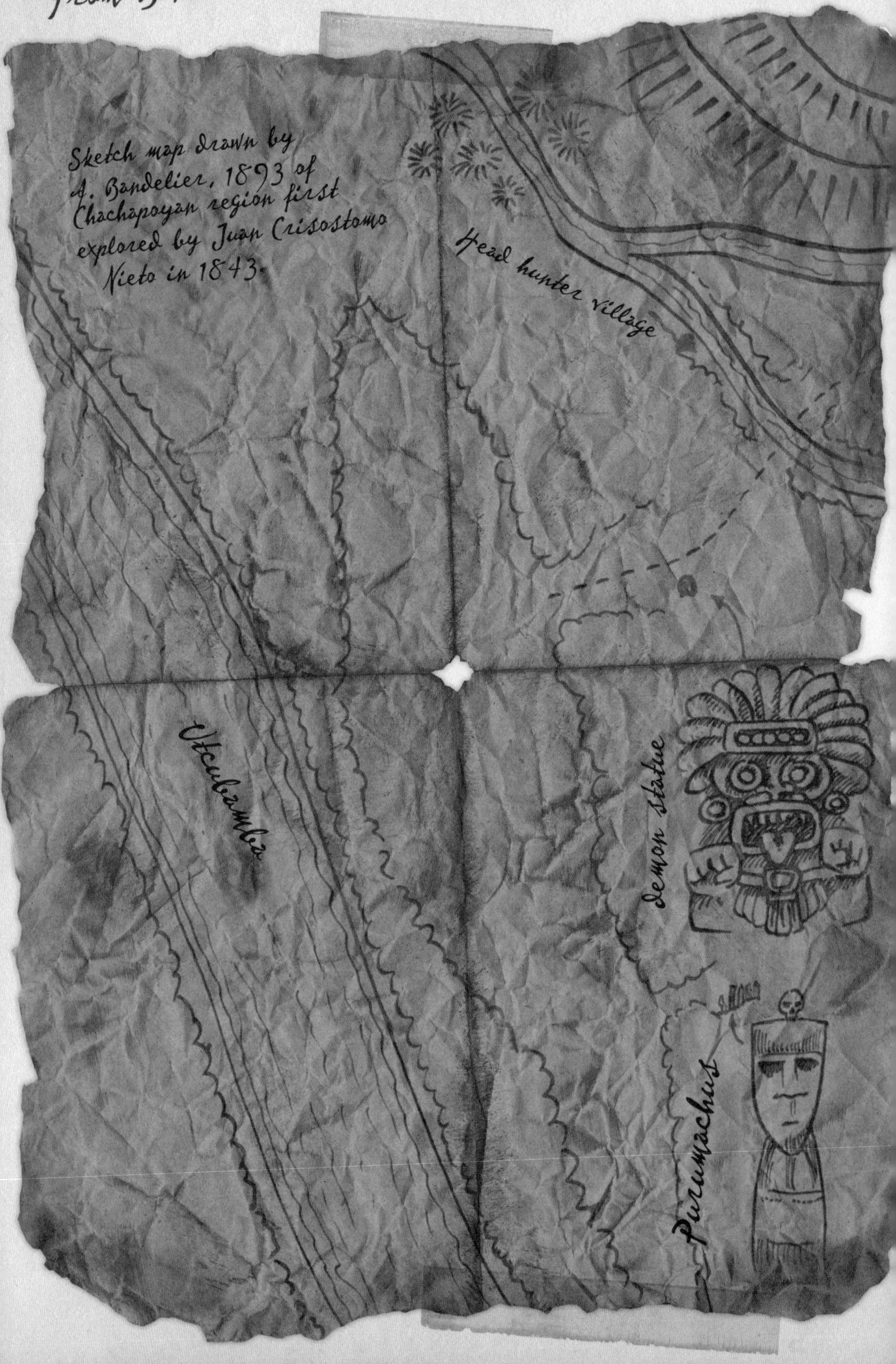
Sketch map drawn by
A. Bandelier, 1893 of
Chachapoyan region first
explored by Juan Crisostomo
Nieto in 1843.
Head hunter village
Utcubamba
demon statue
Purumachus

Paramount peak
of Mt. Shubet

Malca

This large round
chamber must contain
the golden idol.

Found w/ family of porters who "helped" me.
With help like that, who needs enemies?

It seems from his map that Bandelier only explored the entrance of this temple. He notes the tarantulas, but estimated the general shape of the passage and final chamber by structural evidence outside the ruin

Sketch of Chachapoyan Temple
based on my exploration.
Not sure how much
is left of it...

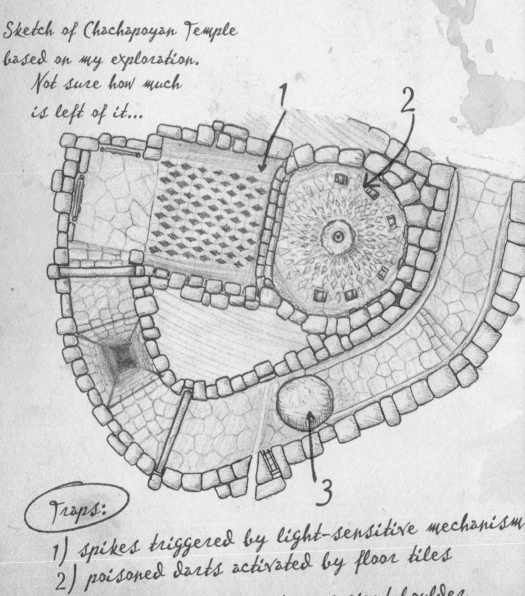

Traps:

1) spikes triggered by light-sensitive mechanism
2) poisoned darts activated by floor tiles
3) weighted pedestal releases giant boulder
   to seal temple entrance

Golden Idol recovered from Chachapoyan Temple
A LOT lighter than it looks! Very similar to the
Tlazolteotl Aztec birthing figure

Must get to Marrakesh to see who is buying the idol from Bellog.
See if Marcus can help fund trip.

SECRET U.S. ARMY

June 12, 1936

To: Col. Musgrove, DOI   CC: Maj. Eaton

The following message was intercepted on 7.9.36 at 13.05GMT:

ENTWICKLUNG IN TANIS LAUFT.
BESCHAFFUNG KOPFSTUCK,

AND:

    STAB DES RA, ABNER RAVENWOOD, US. (lines split but intact)

Translation:
TANIS DEVELOPMENT PROCEEDING. ACQUIRE HEADPIECE, STAFF OF
RA, ABNER RAVENWOOD, US.
        (Trans: EI4)

Cpt. Harrison

Unusual visit from government types after class today. Result: I'm back on the road. Looks like I'll be seeing Abner and Marion again, for better and for worse.

Recommend contact:
Archeologist
Dr. Henry Jones, Jr.
Marshall College
Connecticut

for three days. Then the heralds went through the camp of the children of Israel telling them "And let there be between you and the Ark the space of two thousand cubits: that you may see it afar off." So, here too we see a warning not to approach the Ark. The power of the Ark is more explicitly shown when the Bethsames were slain because they had looked at the Ark (1 Kings 6:19). Likewise, when the ox-cart carrying the Ark faltered, Oza, attempting to steady the Ark, was struck dead after having touched it (2 Kings 6:7).

Strict rules surrounded the Ark. It was to be kept hidden away in the Holy of Holies. Only the High Priest was allowed to enter into this sacred sanctuary, and then only after he had undergone ceremonial cleansing, made sacrifices to atone for his sins and the nation's sins, and burned incense to conceal the atonement cover. When the Ark was moved, it was covered with at least three layers of cloth by the priests to protect others from seeing it and, as mentioned above, everyone else had to keep their distance behind the procession.

Packing list

Hat

Maps

Gun

Notebook

Whip

Glasses cleaning cloth

Toothbrush

Razor (if there's space)

Boots

Abner's Journal

Ark notes

Tickets

THE FEDERAL SECURITY SERVICE OF THE RUSSIAN FEDERATION

NOTE: "Abner's Journal/Ark notes," Dr.
Jones refers to the journal pages sent
to him from Abner ten years prior. Dr.
Jones appears to have been on a U.S.
government mission to recover the Ark
of the Covenant, although why it was
necessary to start his quest in Nepal
is still unclear.

FORM 21-A

Travel Expenses for South America, 1936

Expense record for Marcus

Day 1:
coffee (.05)
newspaper (.02)
lunch (.25)
postcard (.05)
dinner (.50)
lodging ($1)

Day 2:
guides $10
donkey ($5. I think)

Day 3:
Ah, forget it.

PAN AMERICAN AIRWAYS SYSTEM
& Associated Carriers
CONTRACT TICKET — Not Transferable
Not Valid Unless Officially Stamped on Back by Selling Agent
IDENTIFICATION COUPON

The Passenger's attention is called to the terms, conditions and provisions stated and referred to on the back hereof and on baggage check and to the current published rules, regulations and tariffs of the Carrier, all of which are a part of this Contract. Each of the attached Flight Coupons, if officially stamped, when presented attached hereto, will be good for one said passage by the Passenger named below from and to airports at or into the place and in the service of the Carrier thereto respectively named, and to places to which reservations shall have been made, but subject to the above mentioned terms, conditions, provisions, rules, regulations and tariffs.

MR __HENRY JONES JR.__
(Print Passenger's Name)

ROUTING: One Way ☑ Circle ☐ Round Trip ☐

__SAN FRANCISCO__
(Origin)　　　　　　(And other intermediate schedule)

(stopping places)

FARE $ __951.60__　　EXCH. (Destination)
　　　　　　　　　　CY RATE............CY
PASSAGE MUST __10-22__ 19 __36__ FREE BAG
BE COML'D BY　　　　　　ALL'ANCE X ....Ks

CTC No ....　GRB No.............
ISSUED IN CON-
NECTION WITH FORM　　No ....

ISSUED BY PAN AMERICAN AIRWAYS, INC.
AT PLACE AND ON DATE OFFICIALLY STAMPED ON BACK

c21138

Form A, | AGENT OR REPRESENTATIVE _AJ_

PAN AMERICAN AIRWAYS SYSTEM
& Associated Carriers
FLIGHT COUPON — Not transferable

If attached stamped, this flight Coupon when presented attached to the Identification Coupon, is conditional with which it was issued, subject to taxes, conditions, carriage, rules, regulations and tariffs therein stated and therefore, will be Good for One Passage by the Passenger Aforementioned, on planes on which reservations shall have been made, in the service of the following named Carrier and address of which is the point of departure hereunder stated below.

FROM __SAN FRANCISCO__

TO __KATHMANDU__

VIA __HNL   AWK   MNL__

COMMENCING　(Put Name of Carrier)
ON __7-22__ 19 __36__ FARE BAG.
　　　　　　　ALLOWANCE __00__ Kg

ROUTING: One Way ☑ Circle ☐ Round Trip ☐

__SFO__　　　　__HNL__
(Origin)　　　　　　　　(Routing)
__AWK   MNL   KTM__
(Routing)　　　　　　　(Destination)

(All carriers in sequence on line if more than one)
TOTAL
FARE $ __951.60__　CIC No. ☐
　　　　　　　　CY 9RB No. ☐ ____

ISSUED ON THE DATE, AT THE PLACE AND BY THE CARRIER OR AGENCY OFFICIALLY STAMPED ON BACK

c21138

Form A,　　　Void if Detached

August 1, 1936
Picked Marion up in Nepal, and now we're in Cairo together. She says she's my partner on this search, and I guess she is.

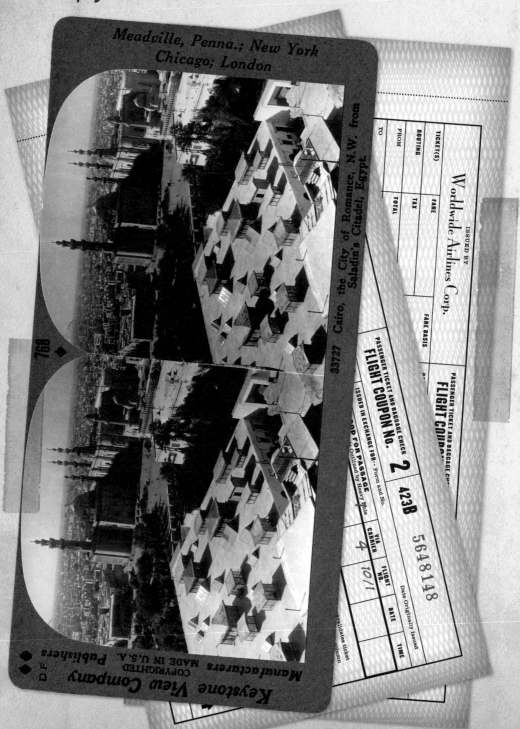

Meadville, Penna.; New York
Chicago; London

33727 Cairo, the City of Romance, N.W. from Saladin's Citadel, Egypt.

Keystone View Company
Manufacturers   COPYRIGHTED   Publishers
MADE IN U.S.A.

768

ISSUED BY
Worldwide Airlines Corp.

PASSENGER TICKET AND BAGGAGE CHECK
FLIGHT COUPON No. 2   423B   5648148

TO
ROUTING
FROM
FARE
TAX
TOTAL
TICKET(S)
FARE BASIS

VIA CARRIER 4
FLIGHT No. 10/1
DATE
TIME
Date Originally Issued

GOOD FOR PASSAGE - Form and No.
Obtained by Heavy Rule
ISSUED IN EXCHANGE FOR-

PASSENGER TICKET AND BAGGAGE CHE-
FLIGHT COUP-

We're staying with Sallah, who I can tell thinks there's something going with us. Ah, so what. Ten years later, and she still looks great. Better, even.

I CAN SEE THE RESEMBLANCE NOW BETWEEN YOU AND THAT MONKEY... —MARION♡

Abner's dead. Marion has his medallion. So it shouldn't be long now until we find the Ark. And then, well, we'll see....

Marion Ravenwood
You shouldn't have come with me.

But there's never any arguing
with you, you do what you want,
always have.

August 2, 1936
Terrible day. Marion died, Belloq's thugs came after
us and I couldn't get to her. I can't even think about
what Abner would do if he were still here. All I
can do is get this thing finished and get out of here
as soon as I can. I've never been so thankful for
good Egyptian liquor.

Last picture I have of her, with the damned monkey on her shoulder. What a rotten day it's been.

Medallion Analysis

The bird shown on the headpiece could be the falcon of Horus.

The large "Eye" atop this falcon is very similar to the crystal in the center of the medallion.

Howard Carter found similar designs among the jewels of King Tutankhamen.

Attachment for headpiece for Staff of Ra. Not of great significance, although the shape is intriguing.

According to Imam, a friend of Sallah's,
the front of the medallion reads:

Feetamah Qamato
  Meaning: "You should
  fear its existence"...
a warning not to disturb
the Ark -but in the
old use this also implies

"six kadam"-72", but the back reads:

  Kabed Yahweh ve ha Meeshkan
  Amah Akhat me Al Kadam

Which translates: "Take back one kadam to honor the Hebrew
God, whose Ark this is"... making the staff 60" or five
feet. Belloq's staff is too long!

Snapshot of medallion, just in case.

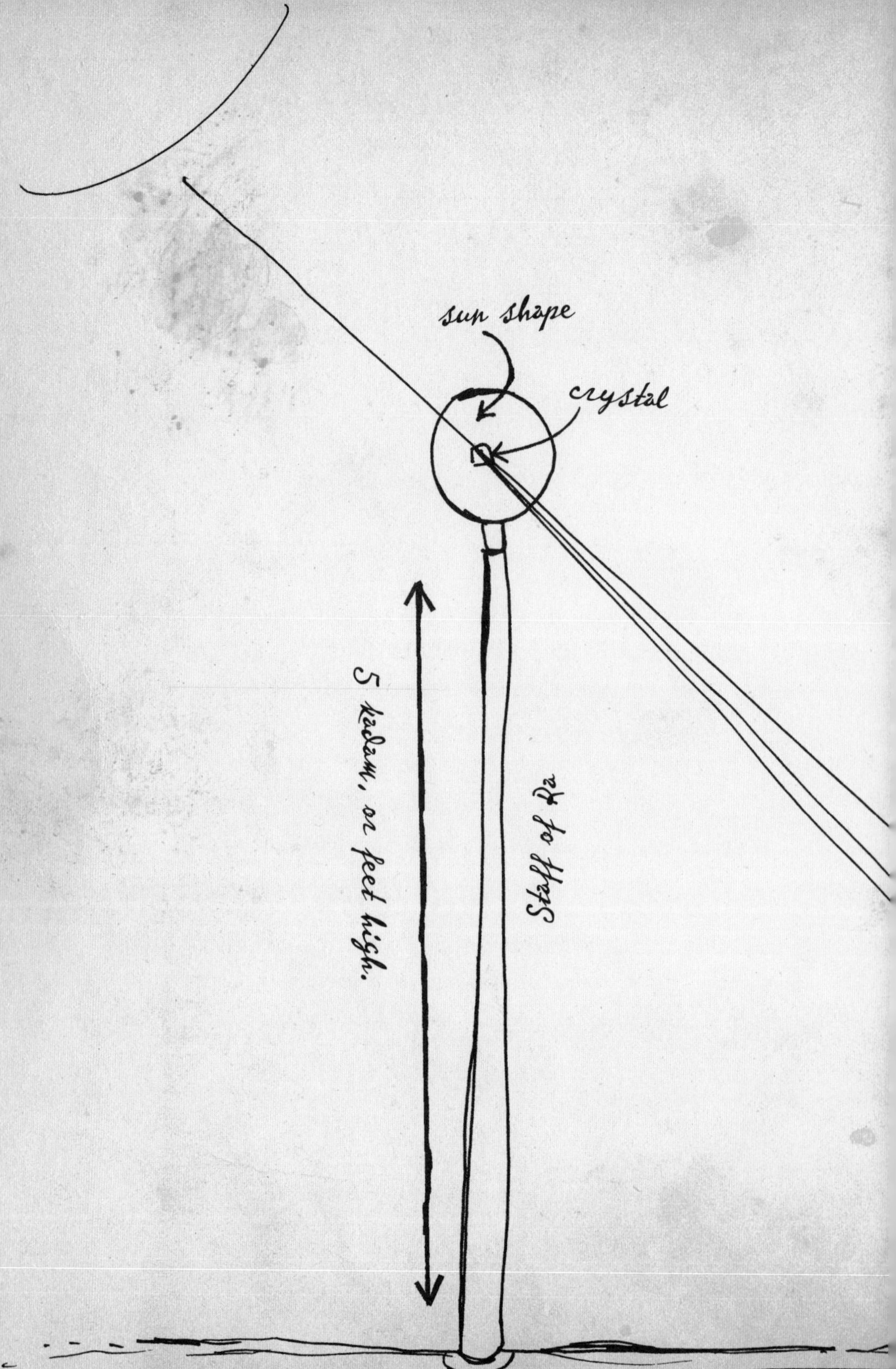

sun shape

crystal

5 kalam, or feet high.

Staff of Ra

Proper location of staff

1. Make a photostat for government agents.

2. Get them copy of the Bible.

3. Sign it from Marcus.

 THE FEDERAL SECURITY SERVICE OF THE RUSSIAN FEDERATION

NOTE: Diagram denotes how Dr. Jones discovered the location of the Ark of the Covenant. Clearly, he found his way to the Map Room in the lost city of Tanis.

FORM 21-A

Light shines in, creates beam through crystal, pointing to location of the Well of Souls

miniature Tanis

Well of Souls

Found this, discarded in the map room by my French friend.

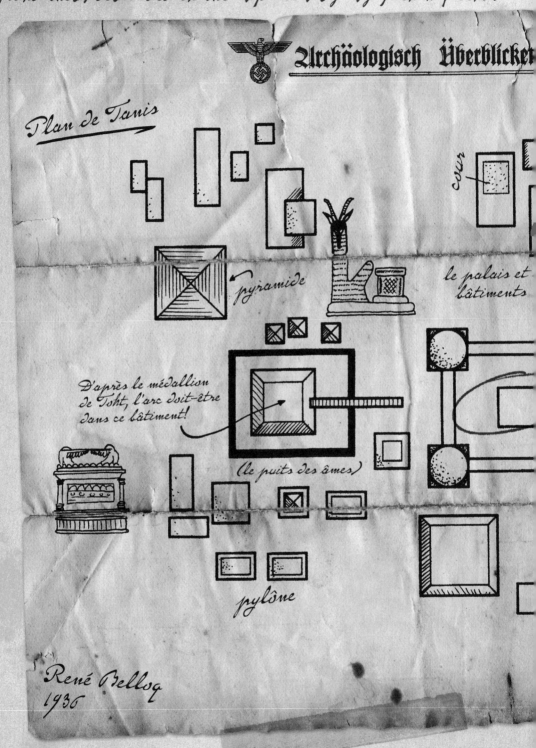

Archäologisch Überblicken

Plan de Tanis

pyramide

cour

le palais et bâtiments

D'après le médaillon de Toht, l'arc doit-être dans ce bâtiment!

(le puits des âmes)

pylône

René Belloq
1936

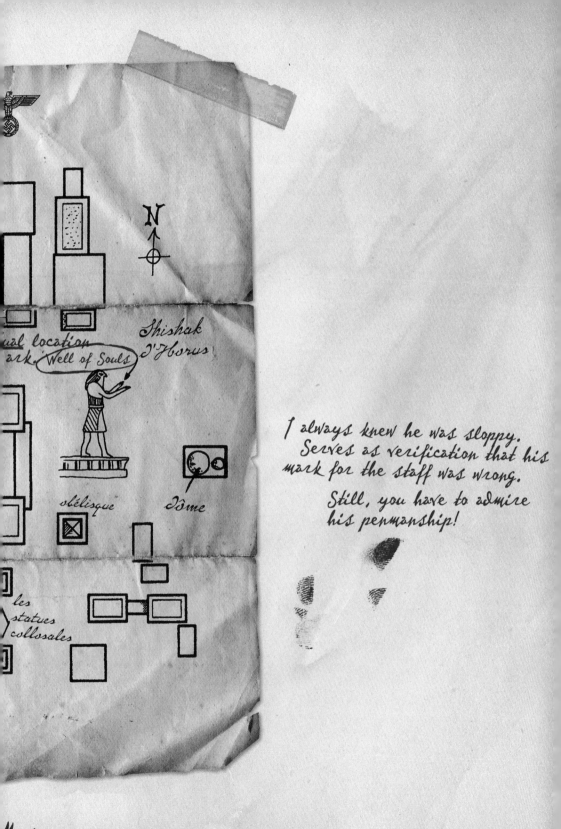

...al location
...ark. Well of Souls

Shishak
d'Horus

obélisque

Dôme

les
statues
collosales

I always knew he was sloppy.
Serves as verification that his
mark for the staff was wrong.

Still, you have to admire
his penmanship!

Marion is okay, it turns out, so things are looking up all around!

The opening of the Ark of the Covenant.

Belloq recited this prayer in Aramaic as he opened the ark (colored sketch at right). I think it was the last thing he ever said. Marion and I missed most of the action, thankfully.

לא על אנש רחיצנה

ולא על בר קלהין סמיכנא

דהוא קלהא קשוט

ואוריתה קשוט

בה אנא רחיץ

ולשמה קדישה יקירא

תשבחן.

Translation:
Not in human do I trust
And not on any child of God do I rely
In him (who) God is true
And whose Torah is true
In him I will trust
And to his name holy precious praise

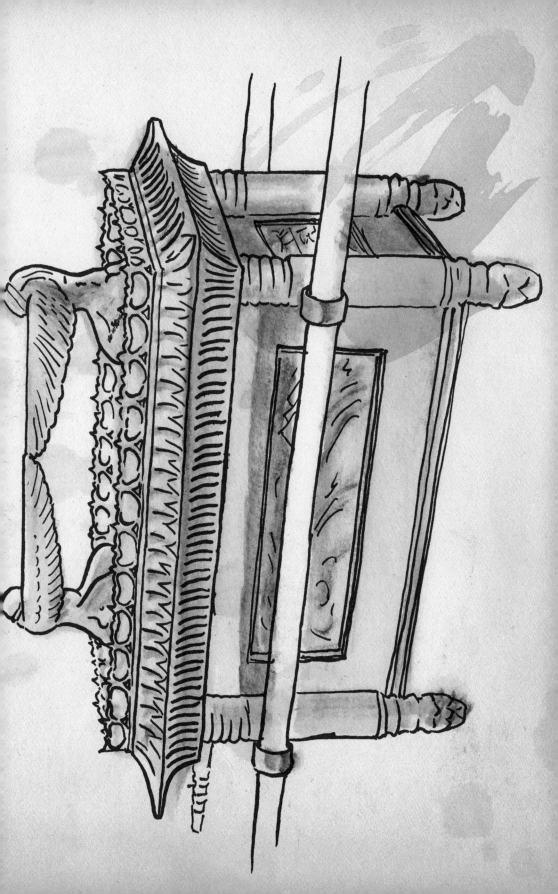

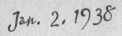

Jan. 2, 1938

After all these
years, finally
recovered the Cross of
Coronado. Anxious to do
a full work-up on it.
It's smaller than I
remember, and heavier.

1938
Auto Driver's License

This License Expires
December 31, 1938

1249983

Issued to   **HENRY JONES, JR.**
Street Address   **38 ADLER AVENUE**
City or Town   **FAIRFIELD**

Age **39**   Weight **180**   Color Hair **BRN**   Color **W**
Sex **M**   Height **6 0**   Color Eyes **BRN**   Fee $3.00

Signature of Licensee   *Henry Jones, Jr.*

This certificate must be carried by the Licensee when operating a motor vehicle.

JONES, H. JR.

Lost my license in an unplanned swim off the coast of Portugal.
Unbelievably, someone fished it out and mailed it back to me.
Good thing, too. I've already replaced it five times. I'm keepin
it taped here from now on for safekeeping.

January 15, 1938

This form shall serve as a confirmation that the museum is processing your payment.

Recipient: Henry Jones, Jr.
38 Adler Avenue
Fairfield, New York

Honorarium: $1,000, plus expenses
[Please submit expense report under separate cover]

For: Cross of Coronado

Policy: Accounting shall pay within 30 days.

It is a lovely jewel, isn't it?
Whatever shall you look for after this coup de grâce!
—Marcus

THE CROSS OF CORONADO—OFFICIAL ARCHEOLOGICAL ANALYSIS
DR. INDIANA JONES

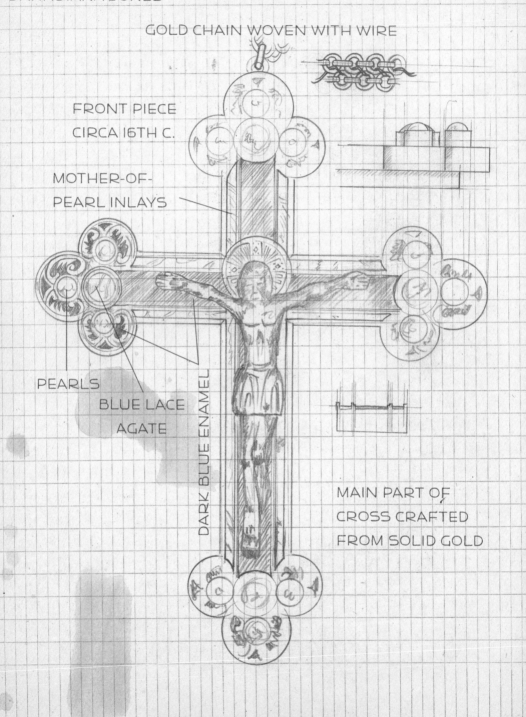

GOLD CHAIN WOVEN WITH WIRE

FRONT PIECE
CIRCA 16TH C.

MOTHER-OF-
PEARL INLAYS

PEARLS

BLUE LACE
AGATE

DARK BLUE ENAMEL

MAIN PART OF
CROSS CRAFTED
FROM SOLID GOLD

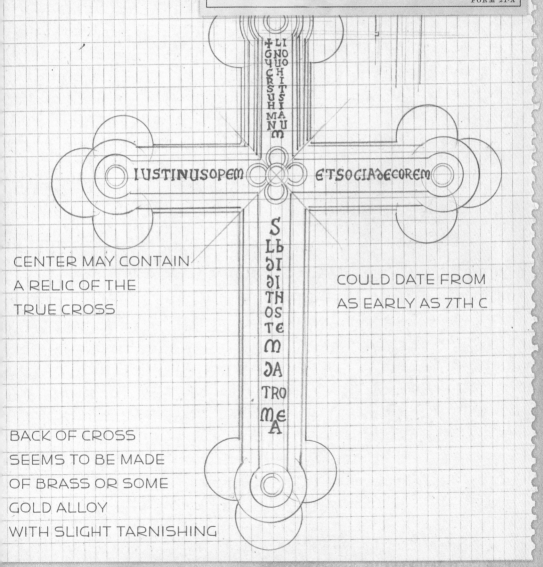

THE FEDERAL SECURITY SERVICE OF THE RUSSIAN FEDERATION

NOTE: The Crux Vaticana, made of bronze and bedecked with jewels, dates from the sixth century and was a gift of the Emperor Justinian II to St. Peter's Basilica in Rome, where it still resides.

FORM 21-A

DEEPLY ETCHED GROOVES

IUSTINUSOPEM ETSOCIADECOREM

CENTER MAY CONTAIN A RELIC OF THE TRUE CROSS

COULD DATE FROM AS EARLY AS 7TH C

BACK OF CROSS SEEMS TO BE MADE OF BRASS OR SOME GOLD ALLOY WITH SLIGHT TARNISHING

Dear Junior,

      Here is my Grail Diary. Guard it with your life and keep it safe. I hope to be able to retrieve it from you soon.

                    Your Father,
                    Dr. Henry Jones

Prof. Indiana Jones
Barnett College
Hamilton Hall
Grove Avenue
Fairfield, New York

From Dad's office. I've looked at it so much I've
memorized every detail, but just in case...

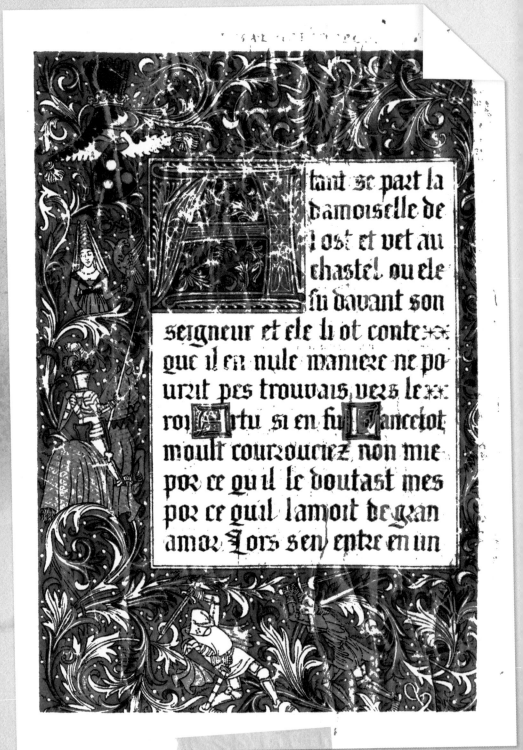

tant se part la damoiselle de l ost et vet au chastel ou ele fu davant son seigneur et ele li ot conte que il en nule maniere ne pourzit pes trouvais vers le roi Artu si en fu Lancelot moult courzouciez non mie por ce qu il le doutast mes por ce quil lamoit degran amor Lors sen entre en un

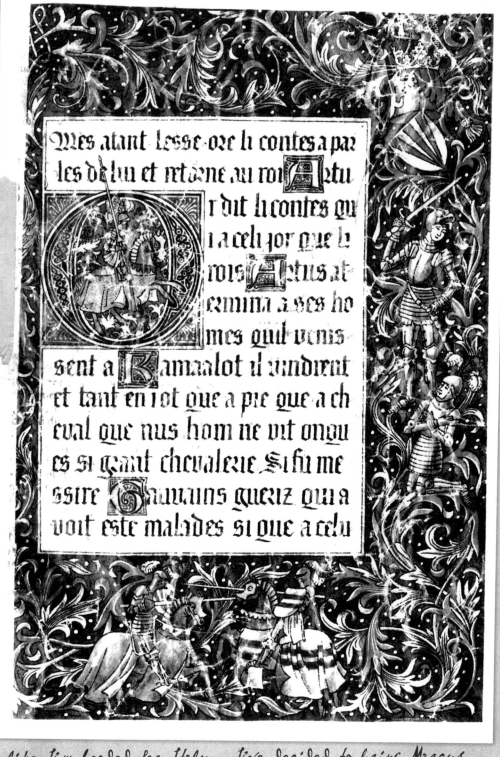

Mes atant lesse ore li contes a par
les de lui et retorne au roi Artu
r dit li contes qu
i a cel jor que li
rois Artus at
ermina a ses ho
mes quil venis
sent a Kamaalot il vindrent
et tant en i ot que a pie que a ch
eval que nus hom ne vit onqu
es si grant chevalerie. Si fu me
ssire Gauuains gueriz qui a
voit este malades si que a celu

ooks like I'm headed for Italy... I've decided to bring Marcus
ith me. He's concerned about Dad and wants to help.
I have a sinking feeling I may regret it. Seems
like I always do when I don't travel alone.

Map of Venice Marcus brought along with us. Maybe it will be a good thing to have a traveling companion again—and Dad will be happy to see him, no doubt.

References.

1. New Great Arsenal
2. New Arsenal
3. Old Arsenal
4. St Peter Patriarch
5. The Verges
6. St Daniel
7. St Ann
8. St Giouchin
9. St Fer. of Paola
10. St Dominic
11. Seminary Ducal
12. St Anthony
13. St Biasio
14. Our Lady of y Arsenal
15. St Martin
16. St John in Bragola
17. The Sepulchre
18. The Piety
19. St Lazhariah
20. Greeks Church
21. St Stefano
22. Commander of the Knights of Malta
23. Little St Anthony
24. St Severo
25. New St John
26. The Little Hospital
27. St John and Paul
28. St Marks School
29. St Giustina
30. The Celestia
31. St Francis of Vigna
32. St Zulian
33. The Capuchin
34. The Begars
35. The Wonders
36. New St Mary
37. St Cantian
38. St Apostles
39. St John Chrisostr
40. St Sophia
41. The Jesuits
42. St Catharines
43. St Felice
44. Priory of the Mercy
45. The Mercy
46. St Marcilian
47. Our Ladys of Orto
48. The Magdalen
49. St Marcuola
50. St Lunardo
51. St Jeremiah
52. St Moyse
53. The Reformed
54. St Gerolamo
55. St Agope

56. Our Lords Body
57. St Lucia
58. St Simon
59. St John Beheaded
60. Orio St John
61. St Stae
62. St Marys Dom
63. St Cassan
64. St William Rialta
65. St John Rialta
66. St Mathew
67. St Aponal
68. St Silvest.
69. St Paul
70. St Augustus
71. St John Evangelist
72. St John Evangelist Church
73. St Stin
74. St Nicholas
75. St Rocks Church

Library

The library where Dad was last seen is circled—that's where we'll start. Ahhh, Veni

NOTE: From the previous pages, we've deduced that Dr. Jones the senior was in peril, hence prompting Dr. Jones the junior's trip to Italy. Intriguing that he began searching for his father in a library, of all places. This seems to be a quirk unique to academics.

FORM 21-A

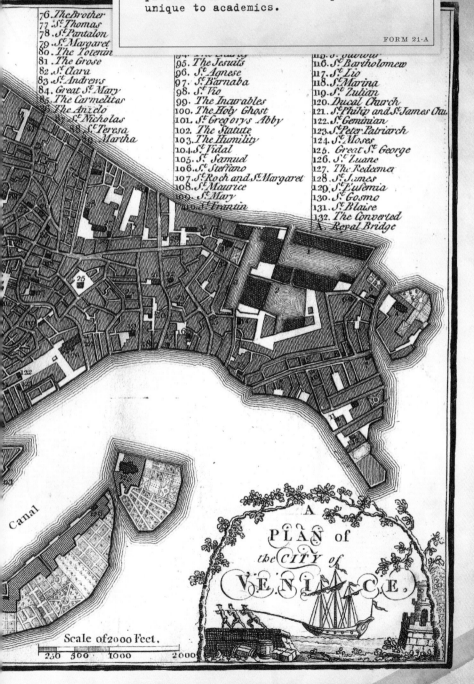

76. The Brother
77. St Thomas
78. St Pantalon
79. St Margaret
80. The Totenin
81. The Grose
82. St Clara
83. St Andrews
84. Great St Mary
85. The Carmelitas
86. The Anzelo
87. St Nicholas
88. St Teresa
89. St Martha

94. The Charity
95. The Jesuits
96. St Agnese
97. St Barnaba
98. St Vio
99. The Incurables
100. The Holy Ghost
101. St Gregorys Abby
102. The Statute
103. The Humility
104. St Vidal
105. St Samuel
106. St Steffano
107. St Roch and St Margaret
108. St Maurice
109. St Mary
110. St Trantin

115. St Sutton
116. St Bartholomew
117. St Lio
118. St Marina
119. St Zulian
120. Ducal Church
121. St Philip and St James Chu.
122. St Geminian
123. St Peter Patriarch
124. St Moses
125. Great St George
126. St Zuane
127. The Redeemer
128. St James
129. St Eufemia
130. St Gosmo
131. St Blaise
132. The Converted
A. Royal Bridge

Canal

A PLAN of the CITY of VENICE.

Scale of 2000 Feet.
250 500 1000 2000

For him we have all the elements of the final storey. This stained glass windows is the final key to the mystery. The monuments must be the clue which we have been searching for in vain...

III

VII

X

the stained glass windows that requires further research

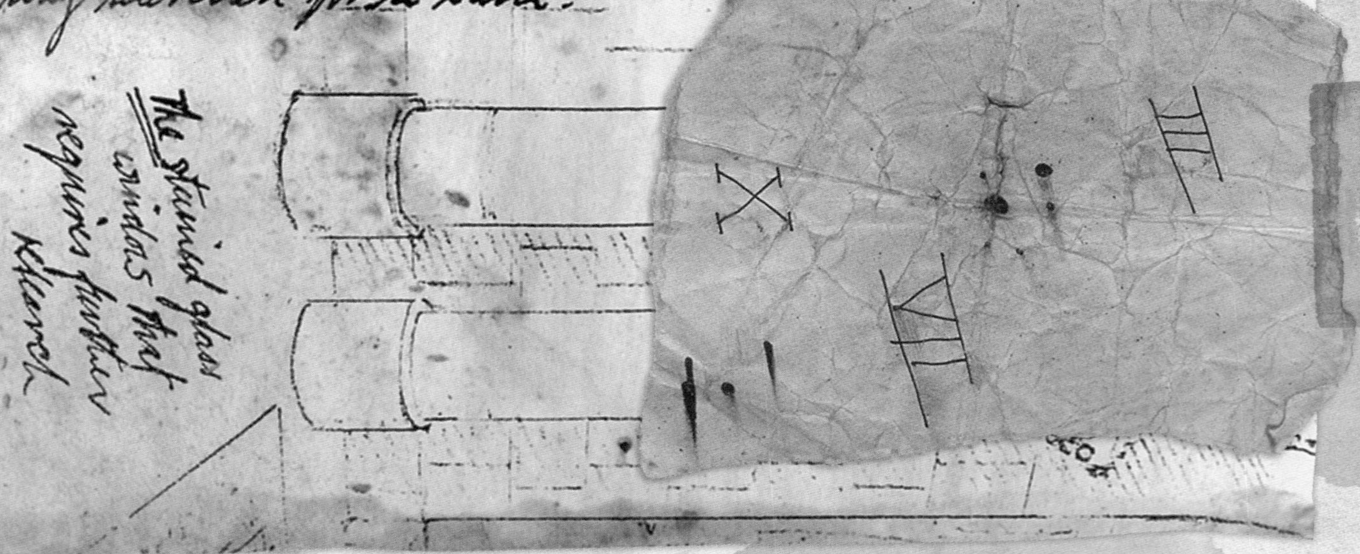

The twins referred to by the knights

Pages from Dad's diary.
Must reevaluate my theory on X's.

part of stained
glass window in
Venice 14th C.

a part of the Franciscan friar's manuscript
mentions the knights of the Grail...
possible link?

Note the
crosses
on the
shield

VII.

words in Latin
note fig 7 ... marker?

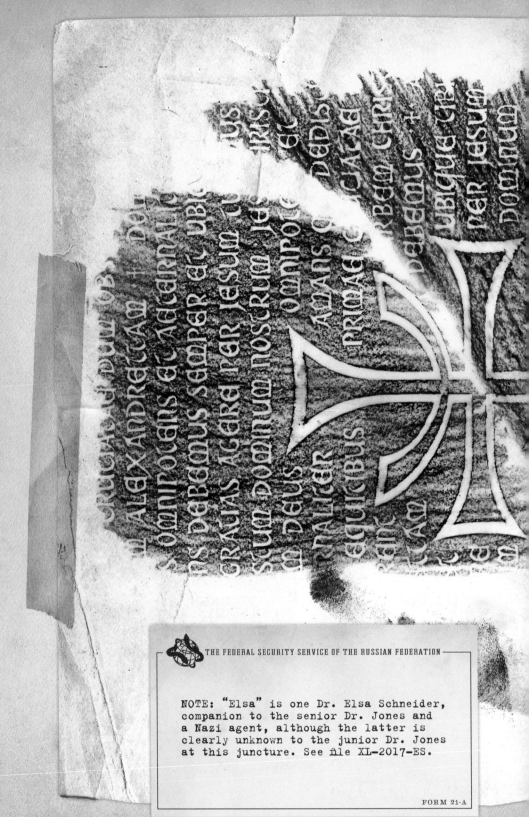

Got this rubbing with Elsa's help.
        Ran into some rats and almost drowned in the process.

...vitae? victimae? fugit
Rex eborum noscri...
in aqua tua dominum
saeculorum sum
repulium eric
veritatem + sine
+ tu deus es meum
itta tuam lucem es
em i sinchae mihi ducas
dicant me ad
m sacram honorem in loco quem incolis per
custas crescentis lunae uni viro satis jacas
templum solis omnibus viris satis sanctum
+ ubi gradalis quae condnet sanguinem iesi
beati illi qui habitant
laudant eum in saecula
isi noscri remanet in aeternum
(um solis omnibus viris satis sa...

Translation ⟶

The full translation of the Grail Tablet rubbing, including the upper portion from the shield is:

...Knights of the First Crusade, while besieging the city of Alexandretta + Lord... God, Almighty and Eternal... we owe love always and wheresoever...
to give thanks to Thee through Jesus, Thou, O God... Through Christ Our Lord, Jesus Christ... Almighty God and... Eternal... loving who you gave to the Knights of the First Crusade... while besieging the city of Christ, Alexandretta, we owe + water... always and everywhere there... to give thanks through Jesus... Our Lord... who drinks the water...
I shall give him, will have a spring inside him welling up

eternal life... O Lord, King of our severe gods... blessed are they who dwell in thy temple, O Lord... they praise you for all time... You, God, are my refuge : Send forth Thy light and Thy truth + These shall be my guide : They shall lead me to Thy holy mountain in the place where you dwell : through

the canyon of the crescent (waxing)

moon : narrow enough only for one man... to the temple of the sun, holy enough for all men... + where the Grail that holds the blood of Our

Jesus Christ dwells forever...
God, holy enough for all men...

The tablet makes several Biblical references including Christ's words to the Samaritan woman at the well (John 4) as well as Psalm 42, which is used at the beginning of the Roman Catholic Mass.

Brotherhood of the
   Cruciform Sword— Ran into these guys in Venice.
They've committed to protecting the Grail. I've managed to learn
a few things about them and their symbol.

Mid-12th Century design

double-carved lines
as on Donovan's
Grail Tablet

Similar to Eastern Cross top bar represents the
titulus cruces and the bottom bar the good and bad
thieves crucified with Christ. The slant in the bottom
represents the bad thieves' descent into hell...

THE FEDERAL SECURITY SERVICE OF THE RUSSIAN FEDERATION

NOTE: By "titulus," Dr. Jones means
one of a distinct number of early
Christian churches.

FORM 21-A

he upper and lower bars
f the cross mimic the shape
f the Holy Grail itself!

A much simpler version is tattooed
upon the chests of the members of the
Brotherhood. The bottom beam does _not_
lant . . . perhaps the scale for
balancing good and evil does not exist
r my friends in the Brotherhood?

et another version, much
ruder and cut out of brass or
old, is worn upon the fez of
the guardians.

NUTIZIE

La Gazzett

12 FEBRUARY 1938   ENGLISH EDITION

UGLY AMERICAN ON RAMPAGE
Causes Heavy Damage to Medieval Library

Yesterday afternoon in the library of San Barnaba, an unidentified American tourist began a trail of destruction and violence that culminated in an explosion near the southern docks.

The escapade began inside the library just before closing time. The American apparently smashed through a marble floor tile using one of the library's cordon posts. He then caused a large fire beneath the library, though details are not clear as to how the fire spread so quickly. The fire department believes a gas leak may be partially responsible.

The American escaped his own fire, emerging through a manhole cover in the square in front of the library with an unknown woman. Running from the scene, they proceeded to steal a speedboat, exiting the Canale Grande into the Canale di S. Marco.

They were soon followed by two more speedboats, which began shooting machine guns at the first boat. The boats then rode straight toward two large steamers, the rear speedboat being crushed between the two ships as a tug forced them together. One of the remaining boats was then caught in one of the steamer's large propellers, destroying the small wooden craft completely.

The third boat was seen fleeing the wreckage and returning to the city by one of the smaller canals. The vandals are thought to have already fled Venice, but police are still searching for clues.

STORIA di Venezia

10 Centisimi

I wonder if this is what Dean Kennedy meant by bad publicity.

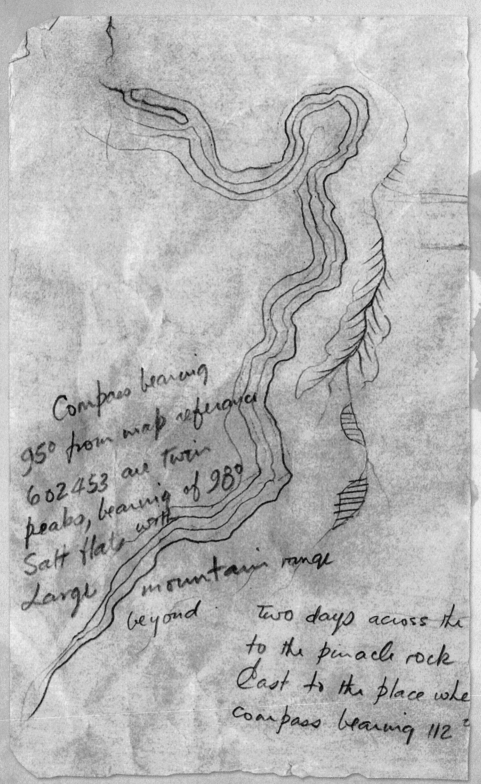

Compass bearing
95° from map reference
6 02453 are twin
peaks, bearing of 98°
Salt Flats with
Large mountain range
beyond.   Two days across the
                to the pinacle rock
            East to the place whe
        compass bearing 112°

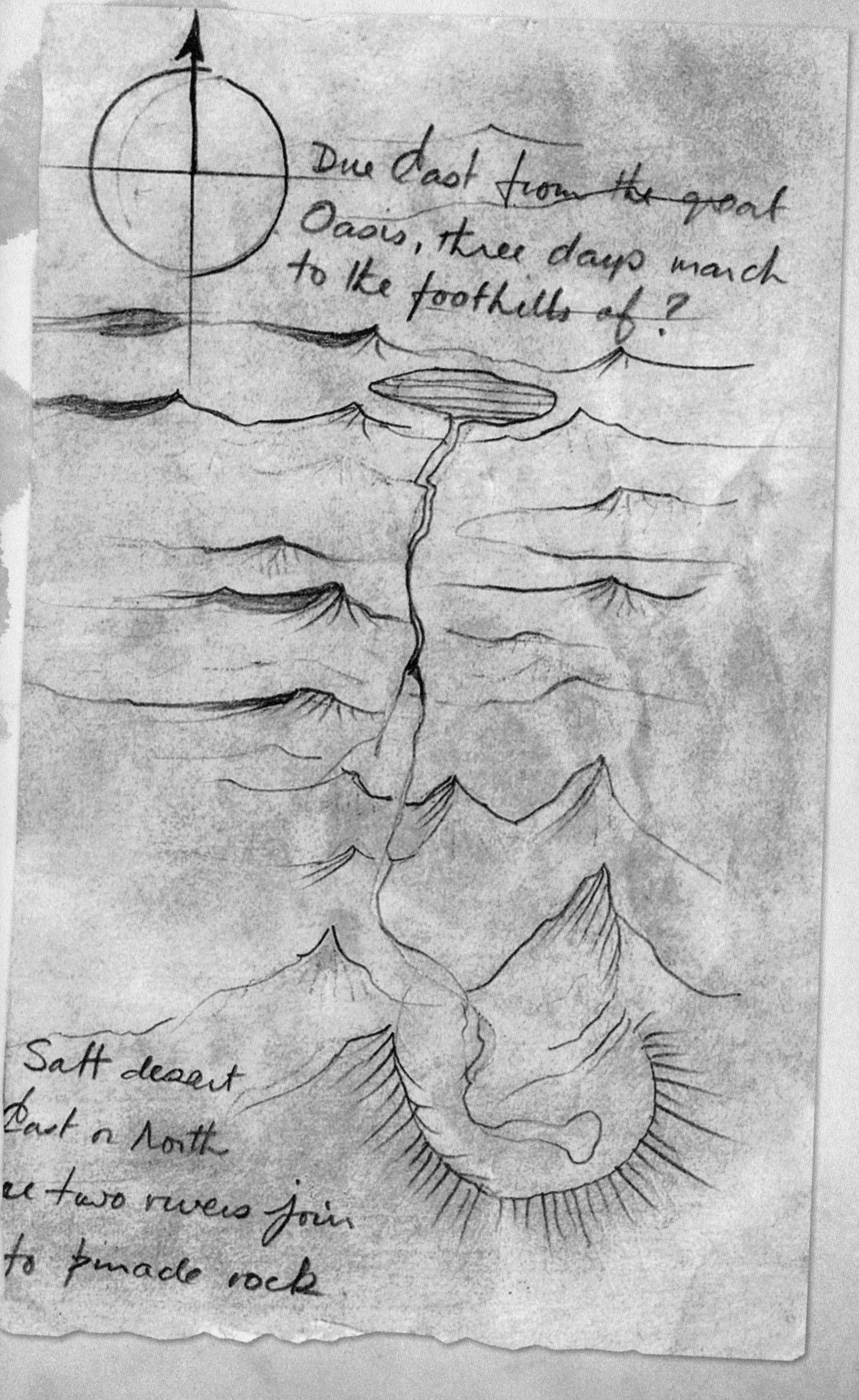

Due East from the great
Oasis, three days march
to the foothills of ?

Salt desert
East or north
... two rivers join
to pinacle rock

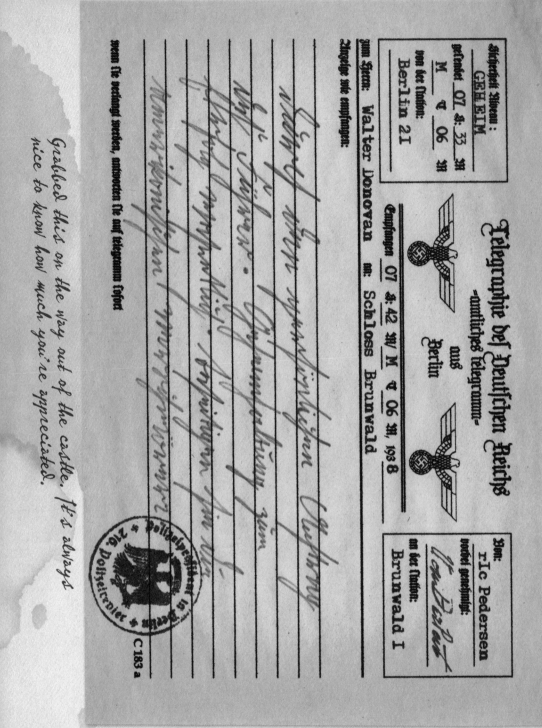

Telegraphie des Deutschen Reichs
-amtliches Telegramm-

Sicherheits Niveau: GEHEIM

gesendet 07 Uhr 33 M
M U 06 M
von der Station: Berlin 21

zum Herrn: Walter Donovan

Zugabe wie empfangen:

aus Berlin

Empfangen 07 Uhr 42 W M U 06 M, 1938
an: Schloss Brunwald

Von: rIc Pedersen
vorher genehmigt:

an der Station: Brunwald I

C 183 a

In English, it reads: "By the personal command of the
Führer. Secrecy essential to success. Eliminate the
American conspirators."
The Germans still have a way with flowery language, I see.

Grabbed this on the way out of the castle. It's always
nice to know how much you're appreciated.

Castle Brunwald.
Used as area Nazi
headquarters.
    Not a terrible place
to be tied up, if you
have no choice.

Fireplace with rotating axel.
Not sure the Nazis knew about it
before Dad and I discovered its versatility.

Copy of snapshot I sent back to a government
friend. Dr. Elsa Schneider, Nazi, associate of
Walter Donovan's. Austrian Grail scholar.

I have reason to believe she's not officially
in bed with Donovan and the Nazis, but just
who _is_ she in bed with?

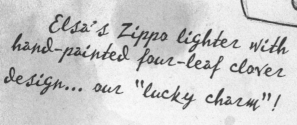

Elsa's Zippo lighter with hand-painted four-leaf clover design... our "lucky charm"!

Gebühren:

.... M. ....Pf.

ngenommen durch:

....

.... mit .... M. 191.... den......../....... um .... Uhr .... Min. ....mitt.

Telegraphie des Deutschen Reichs.

von

Befördert be

.........Uhr ...M.

an ....

burch ....

Telegramm

Frau Dr. Schneiders Anwesenheit

wird unverzüglich in Berlin verlangt.

- Eine Kundgebung am Institut für

Arische Kultur.

- Von höchster Ebene verlangt.

Ansprachen, Viehversteigerungen, patriotische Lieder

Kundgebung der Nationalsozialistischen Partei

Opernplatz, Berlin

4. März 1938

"When one burns books, one will soon burn people."
I hate these guys.

Manifest

der

Kommunistischen Partei.

Veröffentlicht im Februar 1848.

Proletarier aller Länder vereinigt euch.

London..

Gedruckt in der Office der Bildungs-Gesellschaft für Arbeiter

ton D. E. Burghard

46. Liverpool Street

DEUTCHE ZEPPELIN-REEDEREI

BERLIN W8 · FRANKFURT A.M. · FRIEDRICHSHAFEN A.B

DEUTSCHE ZEPPELIN-REEDEREI

FLIGHT COUPON NO. 1

SUBJECT TO CONDITIONS OF CONTRACT

GOOD FOR PASSAGE BY

Name Hr. J. Schotte

mit dem Liftschiff D-138

von Berlin

nach Athen

Bett Nr.	Kajüte	No. des Passagiers
17	B	1

№ 24761138 A

Int. Quittung

DEU

F
SUBJECT TO CON...

GOOD FOR PASSAGE BY

Name Hr. H. Widerstand

mit dem Liftschiff D-138

von Berlin

nach Athen

Bett Nr.	Kajüte	No. des Passagiers
17	B	1

№ 24761138 A

Int. Quittung

Favorite Weapons

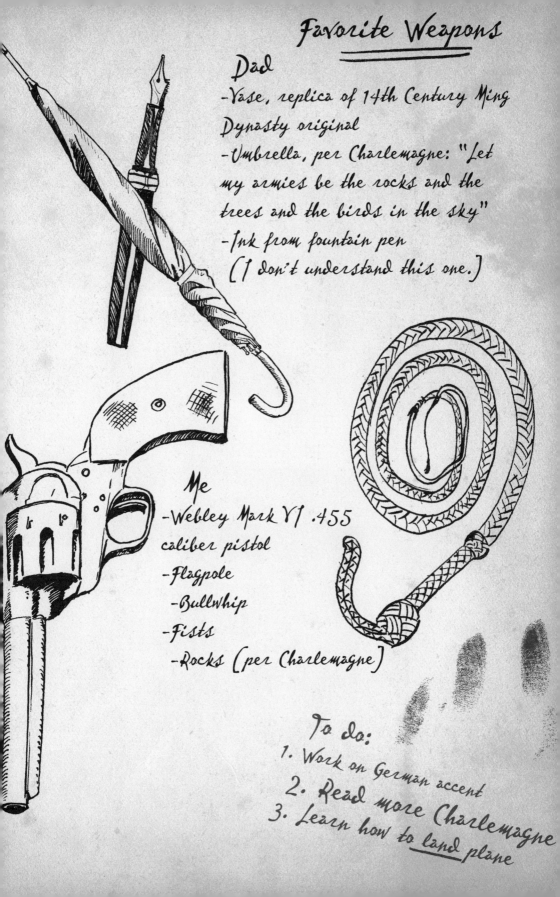

Dad
- Vase, replica of 14th Century Ming Dynasty original
- Umbrella, per Charlemagne: "Let my armies be the rocks and the trees and the birds in the sky"
- Ink from fountain pen (I don't understand this one.)

Me
- Webley Mark VI .455 caliber pistol
- Flagpole
- Bullwhip
- Fists
- Rocks (per Charlemagne)

To do:
1. Work on German accent
2. Read more Charlemagne
3. Learn how to land plane

Zusammenfassung: Während des Fliehens aus seiner Haft wurden ████████████████, Schloß Brunwald ██████████████ ██████████████████████

ᛋᛋ
Gesucht von der Schutzstaffel
Gesucht wegen Verschwörung

Beschreibung

Haar: Braun

Augen: Braun

Größe: 1,83 Meter

Gewicht: 80 kilogramm

Geburtsdatum: 1. Juli 1899

Alias: Indy, Henry, Henri Defense, Heinrich Widerstand, ███████████████

Besondere Merkmale: kinn ████████████████████

Verbrechen: Gesucht wegen Verschwörung, widersetzenden Arrestes, Mordes, ██████████████████

██████████████████████████

Gesucht von der Schutzstaffel wegen Verschwörung

D-8

(Gesucht)

Indiana Jones

Wahrscheinlich bewaffnet und gefährlich
██████████████████████
██████████

Mother would be so proud— matching father and son "wanted" papers. Grabbed these, so only 500 or so more to collect from wherever the Nazis have posted them. I like to think I don't look like that when I travel.

THE FEDERAL SECURITY SERVICE OF THE RUSSIAN FEDERATION

NOTE: "Wanted" papers from the S.S. for father and son. Must have been highly sensitive, given how heavily the text has been censored.

FORM 21-A

geprüft

poſtgel und des
in Sachſen

Urlaubsſchein

Nurgegen Vergütigung des Urlaubſcheiner und des Guit-jarrückſchreiber Gerreichbeſrecht bei der Ur▮▮▮▮▮reiſe beifügich. ▮▮▮▮▮▮ Urlaubsſtelle vrgfälig aufzubewaheren.

Der ▮▮▮▮▮▮▮▮▮ HENRY JONES
(Vor und Zuname)

aus VEREINIGTS STAATEN VON AMERIKA
(Heimatland. Heimatort)

geb. am 6. JUNI 1890 beſchäftigt als DOZENT

iſt vom ▮▮▮▮▮ bis ▮▮▮▮▮ nach ▮▮▮▮▮▮▮ beurlaubt.
(Urlaubsort)

Grund des Urlaubs: UNBEKANNT.
(Fremdtſchemkaut Kammandauteurterſci. Heimatsſtand. beſonders Uſtraße ubw.)

Der Urlauber bei der Arbeiterrückſcheinausweis ▮▮▮▮▮▮ erhalten
von feldmitteln in deutſcher hm. der
betreffenden ausländiſchen Währung geltenden Bet▮▮▮▮▮▮▮▮
Betrieb wieder aufzunehmen.

den 15. MÄRZ 1933

▮▮▮▮▮▮▮▮▮▮
(Armeesgſchaftorps und Unterſchrift)

Beſcheinigung des Arbeitsamts

Der Erteilung des Sichtvermerts zur einmaligen Pass- und Wiedereinreiſt wird zugeſtimmt.

Leipzig den 15. MÄRZ 1938

J. W.
(Unterſchrift)

190660 4.42. C.1136

Dad, on the other hand, never looks any different.

Dad's diary.

I don't know how he hasn't memorized this, especially with how long he's spent looking at it over the years.

Tres numero erunt probationes

(the challenges will number three)

First,

the breath of God —

only the penitent man will pass

Secunda, verbum Dei

(second, the word of God)

only in the footsteps of God will he proceed...

Tertia, semita Dei (third the path of God)

Only in the leap from the lion head will he prove his worth.

Poculum lignarii

(the cup of a carpenter)

The Grail Temple in the Canyon of the Crescent Moon

The three trials of the Holy Grail can be analyzed with three perspectives: spiritual, moral, and historical:

First, the Breath of God; Only the penitent man will pass.

    In the original Latin, "breath" may be "anima" (soul) or "spiritus" (spirit), so the Breath of God may be a reference to the third Person of the Trinity, the Holy Ghost.

The virtue being tested in this trial is that of humility. Only the penitent man will pass. He who is humble and kneels before God will be forgiven from his sins and survive the test.

Historically, this trial is sketched in the diary of St. Anselm, discovered by my father in 1930.
    The mechanical device is shown partially hidden beneath the ground, with a complex series of ropes and pullies. This is the "lethal protective device" mentioned in the lost journal of Paolo of Genoa.

Second, the Word of God; Only in the footsteps of God will he proceed.

    Here, Verbum Dei is clearly a reference to John 1:1, the Word of God, that is, Jesus Christ, the second Person of the Trinity.

In this trial, the virtue of charity is tested.
It is through charity that the Word of God is followed, here represented by literally following the Name of God, the tetragrammaton. In the Latin, the original Hebrew is transliterated as IEHOVA.

    In the chronicle of the Franciscan friar, no more than the name and basic instruction is given for this trial.

<u>Third</u>, the Path of God; Only in the leap from the lion's head will he prove his worth.

Spiritually, the head referenced here represents the source, the primary principle within God, that is the Father.

The virtue being tested here is Faith, the greatest of the supernatural virtues. Only by an act of Faith in God will the questor survive the "leap from the lion's head."

St. Anselm's manuscript also shows a knight seemingly walking on air, passing this trial, the drawing based on an original Medieval painting, now in the collection of my father.

Only by passing these trials, proving one's Faith, Charity, and Humility will one be allowed to approach the Holy Grail.

Here's my rendering of the real deal—the Holy Grail, a simple ceramic goblet—the cup of a carpenter. You'd think Donovan would have known at least that much. But clearly he didn't.

I just hope Dad doesn't get used to tagging along. I think he's had enough.

We lost Elsa. Or rather, she lost herself to her obsession with the Grail. Now she's resting near it, somewhere, forever.

THE LAST CRUSADE

by Prof Henry Jones

A smile. Sort of. Worth noting.... →

The Quest for the Holy Grail is the quest for the divine in all of us. For myself, it has been a forty-year search which reached its zenith in true illumination.

In 1899 I received a vision of sorts, an inspiration to study, from an historic viewpoint, the legend of the Holy Grail. I began my quest by rereading the "fathers" of the myth: Chrétien de Troyes, Robert de Boron and Wolfram von Eschenbach. Each author presented his own version of the tale, the Grail varying in appearance from a bowl to a cup and even a stone.

Though many [...] scoffed at taking the [...] several kept me [...] discoveries across th[...] breakthrough was [...] unearthed near Ank[...] story of Sir Richar[...] who claimed to have [...] Walter Donova[...]

The Quest for the Grail is never truly over. As much for today as for the time of legends, it is a symbol of the unattainable, the eternal.

We are less equipped in these modern times to appreciate the mysteries of the Grail than those men of the Middle Ages. They were nearer, not only in time, to the stories and to what the Grail represents. And it is to these stories that we may turn for even the most tentative illumination.

The Genuine Grail?

There have been but a few ancient chalices that have been reputed to be the Holy Grail. Many scholars believe that the cup from which Christ drank at the Last Supper has already been found, namely in 1910 in Antioch.

Sor[...] tha[...] foc[...] hav[...] the[...] hor[...] for[...] gilo[...] inc[...] a [...] hu[...] sea[...] the[...] of [...] be[...] tw[...] cla[...] th[...] co[...]

S[...] a [...] h[...] e[...] t[...] f[...] i[...] h[...] i[...] c[...]

From the Desk of
DR. HENRY JONES

June 1, 1938

Junior,

I've enclosed a copy of my most recent publication, which I thought you would be interested in perusing. I find myself with a good deal of time on my hands now that the whereabouts of the Grail are known, and am considering taking an editorial position with my colleagues at the Princeton Review. Perhaps we should, as you suggested aboard the Zeppelin, "talk."

Regards,

Your father

PS: I enjoyed our adventures together.

May 1939, Barnett College

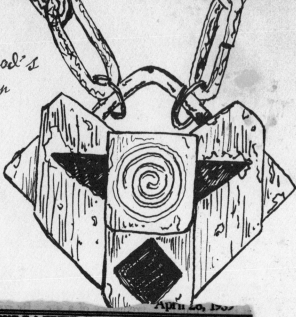

Sophia Hapgood's
copper medallion

She claims a link
between this artifact
and an Atlantean named
"Nur ab sal"

NEWSMAKERS

April 20, 193?

Sophia Hapgood
Noted archeologist who has traded in her pick and shovel for a crystal ball

Bonepicker Turned Mystic Digs For Gold In The Wilds of Manhattan

"Madame" Sophia Hapgood, veteran archeologist of the Jastro Expedition near Reykjavik, Iceland, has seemingly retired from the science of history and entered the realm of the occult.

She is now a for-hire psychic and all the rage in upper society in New York City. She claims to have contact with spirits from the continent of Atlantis with the help of supposed relics from the lost city.

Although most scientists would refute her claims without a second thought, those with money seem more than interested in her supernatural assertions. Some historians, however, do believe that there may be some truth to the myth.

Statue found during the Jastro expedition in Iceland c. 1500 B.C.

Inside the base was a small copper bead

The three stone discs are placed on a center spindle and rotated in various combinations for each entrance. An orichalcum bead is placed in the spindle's mouth. Pushing the spindle operates the ancient mechanism.

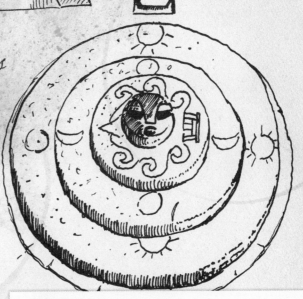

THE FEDERAL SECURITY SERVICE OF THE RUSSIAN FEDERATION

NOTE: Orichalcum is a legendary metal referenced in Plato's "Critius" and alleged to be a key material in the mythical temples of Atlantis.

FORM 21-A

SUPREME HEADQUARTERS
ALLIED EXPEDITIONARY FORCE

Soldiers, Sailors and Airmen of the Allied Expeditionary Force!

You are about to embark upon the Great Crusade, toward which we have striven these many months. The eyes of the world are upon you. The hopes and prayers of liberty-loving people everywhere march with you. In company with our brave Allies and brothers-in-arms on other Fronts, you will bring about the destruction of the German war machine, the elimination of Nazi tyranny over the oppressed peoples of Europe, and security for ourselves in a free world.

Your task will not be an easy one. Your enemy is well trained, well equipped and battle-hardened. He will fight savagely.

But this is the year 1944 ! Much has happened since the Nazi triumphs of 1940-41. The United Nations have inflicted upon the Germans great defeats, in open battle, man-to-man. Our air offensive has seriously reduced their strength in the air and their capacity to wage war on the ground. Our Home Fronts have given us an overwhelming superiority in weapons and munitions of war, and placed at our disposal great reserves of trained fighting men. The tide has turned ! The free men of the world are marching together to Victory !

I have full confidence in your courage, devotion to duty and skill in battle. We will accept nothing less than full Victory !

Good Luck ! And let us all beseech the blessing of Almighty God upon this great and noble undertaking.

Dwight D Eisenhower

June 6 1944

Dear Penelope,

If you get this, it means you have met my mate Indiana Jones, who has come to tell you the bad news about me--if the War dept. hasn't already. When you see Indy--first, don't even think about it. He's not your type! (And a little loyalty for a while would be appreciated, by the way! I like to fancy I'll be mourned for a respectable period.) Second, know that I died doing the right thing, and that I was thinking of you always. Third, after a reasonable time, though I'm clearly irreplaceable, you should try to find someone else and be happy. But not Indiana!

Yours,
Mac

THE FEDERAL SECURITY SERVICE OF THE RUSSIAN FEDERATION

NOTE: "Mac" is Colonel George "Mac" McHale, who seems to have accompanied Dr. Jones through most of the Second World War, including D-Day. See file #79-1331-GM.

"Penelope": unable to find last name. Seems to have had a brief affair with George McHale.

FORM 21-A

COMPLETE FINAL
★ ★ ★ ★ ★ ★
CLOSING WALL STREET PRICES

The

Copyright, 1945, by The

VOL. 112—NO. 205.

Entered as Second Class Matter
Post Office, New York, N. Y.

NEW YORK, FRIDAY

NAZIS SUR
HOLLAND,
AND NO

U. S. and City Agents Seize
Illegal Shipments of Meat

WFA Representatives and Market Inspectors
Take Six Truckloads to Bronx Market
for Inspection.

City and Federal authorities, in raids reminiscent of
prohibition days, cracked down on illegal shipments of
meat coming into the city early today. First reports in-
dicated that thirty-one tons of meat had been seized.

Police detectives, Health and
Markets departments inspectors

$4,000,000,000 CUT

NAZI ARMIES
FALLING APART
IN NORTH AREA

British Stop at Kiel Canal—
Danes Flock to Border
to Greet Allies.

CONFUSION GRIPS THE ENEMY

PASS HALL

Sun

CLOSING
WALL STREET
PRICES

Intermittent rain and continued cool today, tonight and tomorrow.
Temperatures—Minimum, 47; Maximum, 54.
Sun rises 5:51 A. M. Sun sets 7:55 P. M.
(Detailed weather report on page 16.)

1945. **FIVE CENTS EVERYWHERE**

ENDER
ENMARK
TH REICH

TLER STAGED PUTSCH

EISENHOWER TELLS OF CAPITULATION

Battlefield Surrender to Montgomery—Only Armies in Norway and South Still Hold Out.

BULLETIN.

Paris, May 4 (A. P.).—Gen. Eisenhower

'll over now. Or almost. Mac and I were in Flensburg, Germany for the final action. I hadn't been there since I was with Remy n the Great War. It was a little different this time.

"Fake" house designed for A-bomb testing

* Heat rays from nuclear explosion travel at the
  speed of light.
* 3 miles away from explosion: complete destruction
  of all buildings
* 15 miles away: Skin is badly burned
  Many variables affect this, however—such as
  whether explosion is air or ground-based, and what
  meteorological conditions exist.

An eyeful of easier living
by *Wizard...*

Inauguration of
DWIGHT D. EISENHOWER
34TH PRESIDENT OF THE UNITED STATES
JANUARY 20th 1953

Ike is here to stay—for a while, anyway, it seems.

Image and sketch from a recent UFO sighting.

I've seen a few of these myself, though not exactly. Reminds me of Roswell, New Mexico, 1947. And the "Viking" long ship in '39. And the Sky Pirate in '30. Next time, I'll make sure it stays still and says "cheese" so I can get a good snapshot.

I wonder if the Russians have spotted or found similar objects.

Meanwhile, got this sketch from a friend in Washington. Looks like the army is retro-constructing machines based on UFO parts found in Roswell and other places. I'd like a ride when they're done.

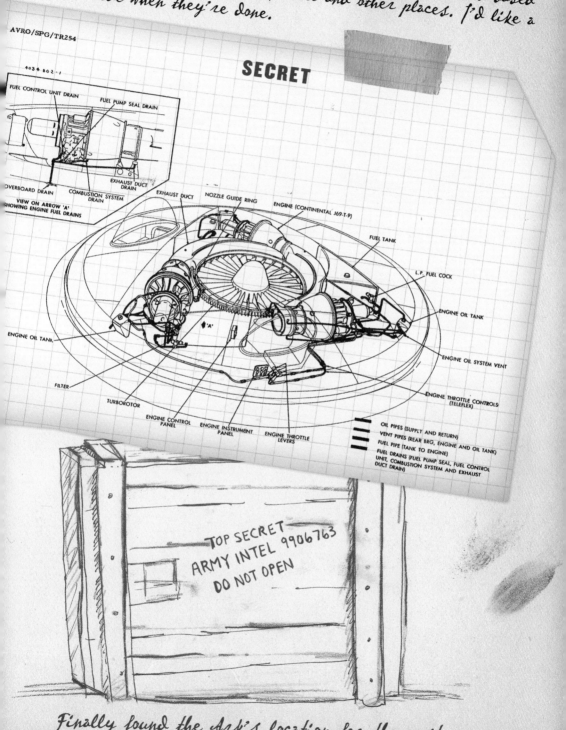

AVRO/SPG/TR254

SECRET

4034 802-1

FUEL CONTROL UNIT DRAIN
FUEL PUMP SEAL DRAIN
OVERBOARD DRAIN
COMBUSTION SYSTEM DRAIN
EXHAUST DUCT DRAIN
VIEW ON ARROW 'A' SHOWING ENGINE FUEL DRAINS

EXHAUST DUCT
NOZZLE GUIDE RING
ENGINE (CONTINENTAL J69-T-9)
FUEL TANK
L.P. FUEL COCK
ENGINE OIL TANK
ENGINE OIL SYSTEM VENT
ENGINE THROTTLE CONTROLS (TELEFLEX)
ENGINE OIL TANK
FILTER
TURBOROTOR
ENGINE CONTROL PANEL
ENGINE INSTRUMENT PANEL
ENGINE THROTTLE LEVERS

OIL PIPES (SUPPLY AND RETURN)
VENT PIPES (REAR BRG, ENGINE AND OIL TANK)
FUEL PIPE (TANK TO ENGINE)
FUEL DRAINS (FUEL PUMP SEAL, FUEL CONTROL UNIT, COMBUSTION SYSTEM AND EXHAUST DUCT DRAIN)

TOP SECRET
ARMY INTEL 9906763
DO NOT OPEN

Finally found the Ark's location for the past twenty years— may have to make a return trip— what else is in that hangar??

September 15, 1957

Dear Dr. Jones,

You won't believe it! I am close to finding the Peacock's Eye! You
know after all this time I keep looking and I keep looking, and it is
in Hawaii! It's on an island they call Niihau, where it's fallen into
hands of natives. Yeah, yeah, no time for love, right Dr. Jones?

     Your friend,
       Short Round

16th Century Conquistadors and their armor— note prep for lecture:

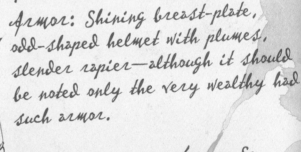

Armor: Shining breast-plate, odd-shaped helmet with plumes, slender rapier—although it should be noted only the very wealthy had such armor.

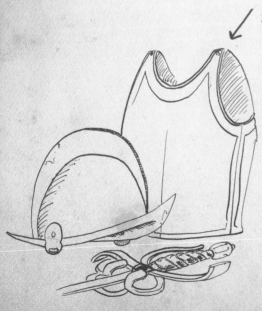

Note for discussion/exam: So often, our common assumptions about what historical figures such as conquistadors look like are guided by a few dramatic renderings, and wholly inaccurate. What other such historical assumptions/images do we hold, and are they accurate?

The RED ARMY CAN BE BEATEN

WE ARE BEING PANICKED BY THREE MYTHS:

1. That Russia is too well armed for us to defeat her in a land war
2. That we can't match her man power
3. That her territory is too vast to be taken

Three nations - Russia, Britain and the U.S.- have exploded nuclear devices. The small dots on map denote A-bombs; large dots, H-bombs.

Scientists estimate that more than 100 atomic and hydrogen bombs have been exploded since 1945. They agree that radioactive fall-out from some of these explosions will continue to menace hun

 THE FEDERAL SECURITY SERVICE OF THE RUSSIAN FEDERATION

NOTE: As we suspected, Dr. Jones had been "interested" in our military capability for some years prior. What else did he know and when?

FORM 21-A

Menu

F. W. W

BACON and TOMATO............40c
Toasted Three Decker Sandwich

BAKED HAM and CHEESE.........45c
Toasted Three Decker Sandwich

CHICKEN SALAD................50c
Toasted Club Sandwich

HAM SALAD and EGG SALAD......40c
Toasted Three Decker Sandwich

PLAIN or TOASTED

BAKED HAM Sandwich..

HAM SALAD Sandwich............25c

EGG SALAD Sandwich............25c

AMERICAN CHEESE Sandwich......25c

HAVE A TREAT

Fountain Features

DE LUXE
TULIP SUNDAE 25c
2 Dippers of Ice Cream cov-
ered with Crushed Fruit or
Fresh Fruits in Season
CHOICE OF
STRAWBERRY, PINEAPPLE, CHERRY,
CHOCOLATE OR HOT FUDGE
Topped with Whipped Topping
and Roasted Nuts

SUPER JUMBO
BANANA SPLIT 39c
½ Banana covered with 3
Dippers of Ice Cream and
Crushed Fruit or Fresh Fruits
in Season
CHOICE OF
STRAWBERRY, PINEAPPLE, CHERRY,
CHOCOLATE OR HOT FUDGE
Topped with Whipped Topping
and Roasted Nuts

EXTRA RICH
ICE CREAM SODA 20c
POPULAR FLAVORS
Made with 2 Dippers of Ice Cream
Crushed Fruit or Fresh Fruits in Season

MALTED MILK.....................25c
Popular FLAVORS   *Made with 2 Dippers of Ice Cream*

MILK SHAKE......................25c
Popular FLAVORS   *Made with 2 Dippers of Ice Cream*

BANANA SPLIT Regular 25c
Popular FLAVORS   *Made with 3 Dippers of Ice Cream*

FRESH ORANGE JUICE ... Regular 12c — Large 24c

HOT NESTLE'S WITH WHIPPED TOPPING......10c
DELICIOUS CHOCOLATE FLAVOR

APPLE PIE ....Per Cut 15c
WITH ICE CREAM.....................20c
LAYER CAKE ....Per Cut 10c
WITH ICE CREAM.....................15c

*Quick sketch of one of the
thugs following us—
-Russian military uniform.
KGB operative
-Tall, thin—maybe 6'0
and 180 lbs.
May have seen him before;
not too bright*

Printed in U. S. A.

Notes for CIA
* Sketch of subject,
  Spalko, receiving the
  commendation of the
  Order of Lenin.
*Tenacious
*Vicious, good with
  a rapier
* Warning: Use great caution
in any dealings with subject

Met juvenile
delinquent. What's
wrong with kids
these days?

Giant ants of the Amazon
- Jaws strong enough to break human sk...
- Size and appearance based on amount o...
fungus they were fed at larval stage
- For the giants, primary purpose is to
retaliate in case of attack
- Most are six inches long
    - Ugly as hell

Jungle Cutter—This cuts through the jungle like a knife through butter, but once things get out of hand, you'd best watch where you stand. The wheels on the front are not exactly a merry-go-round.

City of Gold, with Temple of Akator at center

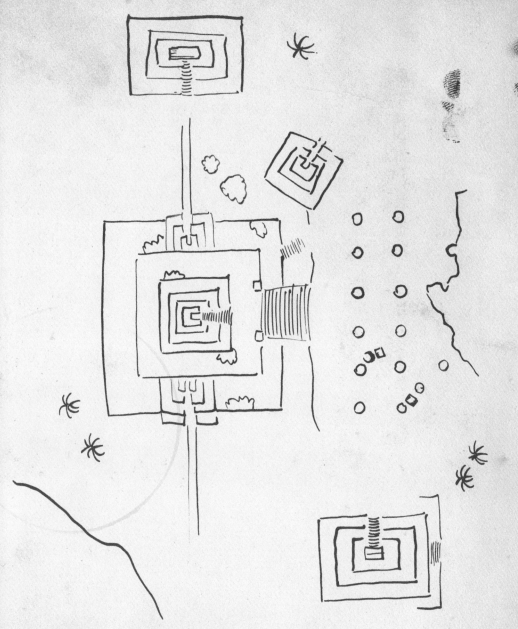

Legendary Ecuadorian city, from the history or mythology
(your pick) of Colombia, ordered to be built by Incan
commander Tupac Yupanqui in the 15th Century. Indians
relayed stories of its splendor to Spanish—temples of gold,
they said—but never seen by Spanish. "Gold" may have been "code"
word for something else...

Nazca Lines, created 200 BC—700 AD

Geoglyphs, these two of a condor and a hummingbird,
but there are over 70 discernable figures.

- Theories on how (Note: shd bring into class assignment)—if you
  could only see from the air, and the Nazca people could not fly—
  how could they see them?
- Theories on why (also for assignment):
  Religious? Artistic? Alien? Other?

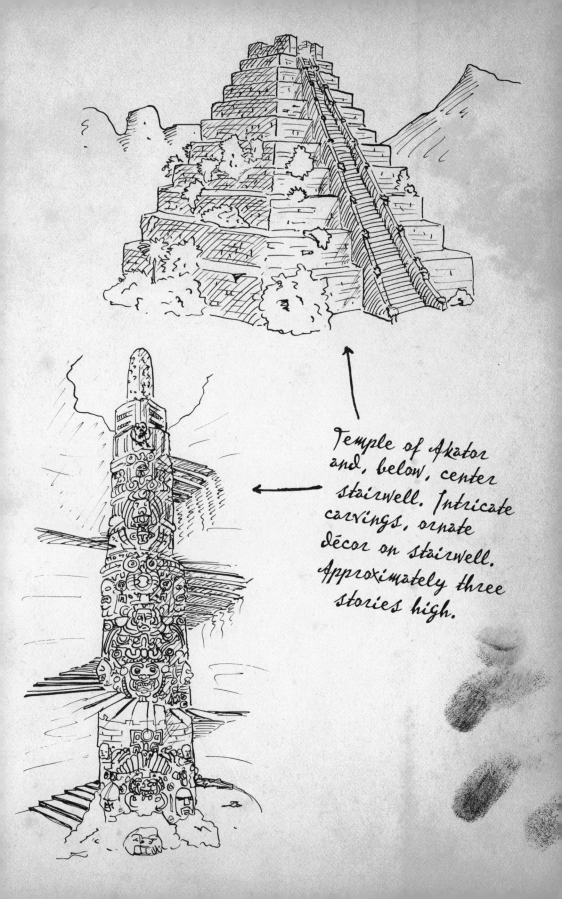

Temple of Akator
and, below, center
stairwell. Intricate
carvings, ornate
décor on stairwell.
Approximately three
stories high.

Azator throne room
4 out of 5 "Crystal" skeleton skulls can be seen;
13 all together. Lucky number!

Conceivably a dozen crystal skulls exist worldwide—it seems like I've searched for half already.

Dimensions:

- 5 inches high, 7 inches long and 5 inches wide.
  - Made from: Clear quartz crystal
- Powers: Reputedly, can grant holder extrasensory perception

Note: no marks, no scratches—leading to much speculation regarding how it was chiseled.

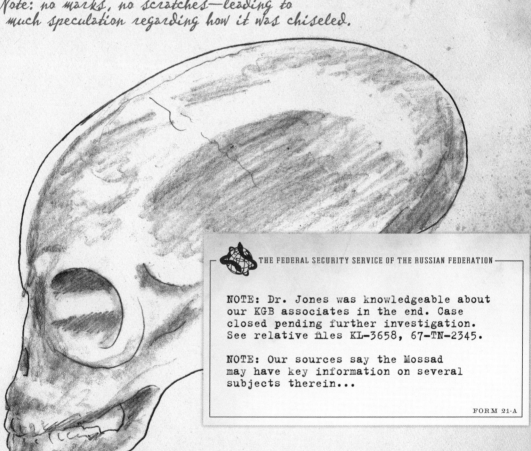

THE FEDERAL SECURITY SERVICE OF THE RUSSIAN FEDERATION

NOTE: Dr. Jones was knowledgeable about our KGB associates in the end. Case closed pending further investigation. See relative files KL-3658, 67-TN-2345.

NOTE: Our sources say the Mossad may have key information on several subjects therein...

FORM 21-A

I've got reason to believe the KGB and certain intelligence organizations are after my journal (like the Nazis were after the Grail Diary—Dad would've appreciated the irony). But I wouldn't want any of this falling into the wrong hands...

Pocket Books, a division of Simon & Schuster, Inc.
1230 Avenue of the Americas, New York, NY 10020

2008 First year of publication

ISBN-10
1-4165-6315-6

ISBN-13
978-1-4165-6315-0

The Lost Journal of Indiana Jones is produced by becker&mayer!,
Bellevue, Washington. www.beckermayer.com

FIRST EDITION

DESIGN: Joanna Price
ILLUSTRATIONS: Anthony "Indy" Magnoli, Kristen Wisehart, Joanna Price
TEXT AND EDITORIAL: Anthony "Indy" Magnoli, Jenna Land Free, Amelia Riedler
PHOTO EDITOR: Shayna Ian
PRODUCTION COORDINATORS: Shirley Woo and Leah Finger

Lucasfilm Ltd.
EXECUTIVE EDITOR: Jonathan Rinzler
ART DIRECTOR: Troy Alders
KEEPER OF THE INDYCRON: Leland Chee
LUCASFILM ARCHIVES: Laela French, Dinah Houghtaling
IMAGE ARCHIVES: Tina Mills, Stacey Leong, Matthew Azeveda

Indianajones.com

10 9 8 7 6 5 4 3 2 1

Printed in China